Georgina Newbery's abiding passion for fashion was nurtured during five years working for American *Vogue* and John Galliano in Paris. Eventually, exhausted, she turned her hand to the less demanding (she thought) task of novel writing. Surprised by the success of her first novel, *Catwalk*, and drawing on her extensive knowledge of the fashion industry, she now writes full time. She divides her time between London and Paris and travels as much of the world as she can on her journeys between the two.

Also by Georgina Newbery

CATWALK

Think Pink

Georgina Newbery

WARNER BOOKS

A *Warner* Book

First published in Great Britain
by Warner Books in 1998

Copyright © Georgina Newbery 1998

The moral right of the author has been asserted.

All characters in this publication are fictitious and any
resemblance to real persons, living or dead, is
purely coincidental.

A CIP catalogue record for this book
is available from the British Library.

ISBN 0 7515 2328 3

Typeset in Perpetua by M Rules
Printed and bound in Great Britain by Clays Ltd, St Ives plc

Warner Books
A Division of
Little, Brown and Company (UK)
Brettenham House
Lancaster Place
London WC2E 7EN

For Lucy, Serena, Sophie and Susan

With many thanks to the usual bunch, especially
Christopher, David and Ian, and of course
Geoff Richards and Mike Pohling
for their constant support.

PART 1

London

Chapter 1

A FREEZING evening in late February did nothing to alleviate the heat in Annabel French's City of London atelier as the final touches were put to her first collection of *haute luxe* ready to wear. She wiped her face with a huge pink cotton handkerchief and tried not to flake too openly. Annabel knew that if she made her team carry on much longer she'd have to take them all out to the Fox and Anchor the other side of Smithfield Market for an alcoholic breakfast. She could see the thought etched on her assistant George's face with painful clarity. She pushed longings for black pudding and whisky aside and tried to concentrate. George was standing ready with a pincushion strapped to one wrist, a tape measure draped around his neck, a kirby grip keeping his fringe out of his eyes and a pair of scissors in his right hand. Annabel's business partner, Duncan Shafe, showed solidarity by sitting in his office, working on their end of year accounts. All the machinists and cutters who worked for her were there too, putting the final touches to a collection they knew was exceptional.

'Right – change the music – can't bear any more of this,' Annabel said of the Van Morrison CD that had been playing for about four hours. 'Let's have some Spice Girls or something before we all fall asleep on our feet.' She turned to the model who'd come for her fitting. 'Pandora, please, we're trying to do a fitting here. Can't your phone calls wait?'

'Darling, you were hardly concentrating.' Pandora Williams blew a kiss at whoever was at the other end of the phone and put it down. 'There you are, Annabel. I'm all yours.' She put her hands on her hips and shook out her waist-length black hair in readiness. She was wearing a skin-coloured G-string and nothing else, but as she knew she had the most beautiful body that anyone there had ever seen she saw no reason to be embarrassed. 'What am I going to wear?'

George came forward with a dove-grey silk velvet dévoré evening dress and slipped it over Pandora's head. She stood stock-still and patient while he arranged the folds of the skirt around her feet and pulled at the shoulders until they clung like a second skin. Annabel took a long silver arrow and wound Pandora's hair into a chignon, pinning it with the jewellery. She and George stood back and admired.

'Can I look?' Pandora was desperate.

'Wait a second.' Annabel circled the model, her expert

eyes searching for the slightest imperfection, the tiniest wrinkle, anything that might mean that her *pièce de résistance* was not perfect. She found nothing. 'Now you can look.' And Pandora turned and stared at herself in the floor-length studio mirror.

'Annabel, I'm speechless. It's divine.'

'No, it's not. There's something wrong with it.' Annabel was circling again, watching as Pandora began to move in the dress, test driving it, seeing what it would do for her, whether she and the velvet would make a good team. The skirt flared around her ankles, the weight of the fabric pulling the dress out in a swirl the colour of dusk over London after a long, hot day.

Duncan took off his glasses and looked at Annabel through the open door of his office. He wished she didn't look so vulnerable when she was tired. He knew she was a budding workaholic and tough as old boots, but in the harsh light of the atelier with her pale hair scraped away from her face and tied back with a scrap of baby-blue fabric, the lines of her cheekbones were sharp and the shadows under her eyes too deep for his liking. Annabel flashed him a look to tell him to stop staring. He blushed at being caught, pushed up his glasses and turned back to his spreadsheets. Annabel might have her first show in two days, but for Duncan the fifth of April was not far off and the first collection was not the only thing that had to be shown. He was desperately trying to make their first year's losses fit into the business plan he and Annabel had put together when she'd left St Martin's the previous summer.

Annabel stamped her foot in frustration.

'What's the matter with it?' Pandora laughed and swirled again. 'How could you possibly think there's anything wrong with this? Look, it's so beautiful I wish I could remember a bit of Shakespeare to describe it with.'

George was determined to get some sleep that night. Annabel must be persuaded to let the collection go for a few hours. 'Annabel, it's fine. The story works; the narrative of the collection makes sense. There's nothing there that doesn't need to be, and you have enough to show to make a respectable first presentation. I really don't think there's anything more we can do.' He sagged onto a high atelier stool and prayed she would let them all go home. Surreptitiously, he sniffed an armpit and let his mind drift from huge fry-ups to thoughts of showers. The thirty outfits which art student and model friends would wear down the catwalk in two days' time were fitted on mannequins and lined up against a wall, the storyboard of the collection pinned behind them. Each piece had been painstakingly researched, each fabric was specially made, each piece of clothing stood perfectly on its own or as part of the look of the season.

'Oh be quiet, George,' Annabel snapped. 'I'm thinking.'

George shrank back, chastened.

Annabel was a perfectionist and something was bothering her. She couldn't quite see yet where the problem lay, but she had to find the clashing element which was ruining the collection, and until she found it she was afraid that everyone would just have to wait with her. They could sleep in April when it would all be over, and not before. Except for Pandora. Her phone rang.

'Hello, sweetie – no, I've finished here. I'm wearing the most divine thing you ever saw and you've got to shoot me in it as soon as the show's over. I promise, it's the dress of the season.' There was a pause 'No, nothing in Paris is going to be as good as this.' She giggled. 'Don't tell Cristo, he'll be furious. He's going to have to do one of his Grand Master supporting the new boys acts with Annabel. You know how he hates that.'

Pandora threw her phone into her bag and turned to George, arms high in the air so that he could take the dress off her. 'I can go, can't I, Annabel? And you should let all these people go too. It's not fair to keep them here when everything's already perfect.' She slipped out of the dress and was dressed in her own Chanel twinset and skinny pants and out of the door before Annabel had had time to react.

'Oh, go on then, everyone, go home.' Annabel's gesture of largesse swept all her staff into a flurry of activity as they downed tools and grabbed their belongings, desperate to go before she changed her mind.

As George slammed the door behind him, leaving only Duncan to keep Annabel company, the telephone rang.

'Mimi! Thank God it's you!' Duncan relaxed behind his computer screen and watched as Annabel settled into a conversation with her best friend.

'How're you doing?' Mimi asked.

'Something's the matter and I can't put my finger on it and it's driving me mad. I've just let everyone go home. The atelier was full of people wondering what on earth's wrong with me and if they'll ever get any sleep, and George kept waving his scissors at me threateningly. I wasn't sure if he meant to commit hara-kiri or murder. I thought it was time to get rid of him before it got bloody. Honestly, these people have no stamina. You know, he had the nerve to ask me for a pay rise earlier. I could have shot him. He's an assistant, for God's sake – he's been working for less than a year. What does he want the money for anyway? He lives at home – his mother feeds him – and he's working for the next big fashion star. What more could he want?'

'Calm down, Annabel, and stop being horrible about the poor boy. He probably just doesn't want to live with his mother. You wouldn't, would you?'

'Stop being so fair, Mimi. Anyway, my mother's different.'

'Understatement.' Annabel could hear Mimi shift into bossy calming mode from the other side of the Atlantic. 'Annabel, you can't go on like this. You're not making sense. Give George a pay rise after the collections, and now that you've sent them all home, go home yourself. Everything will be much clearer in the light of day.' Mimi sounded efficient and annoyingly awake from her office in New York.

Annabel looked at her watch. It would be the end of Mimi's working day soon and she could see no end to hers. 'But we've so little time,' she wailed.

'So there's not much you can do anyway. Go home. You'll realise what the problem is tomorrow. Come in early before everyone else and look at it all in daylight. You'll see whatever it is right away.'

'Maybe. When are you coming?'

'My flight leaves tomorrow morning. I'll be with you by midnight. Is Antonio there?'

'Yes, and he's being such a darling taking my mind off things.'

'Can I talk to him?'

'Oh, he's not here. God, no. Antonio in the atelier? I'm not sure he even knows where it is. This would bore him silly. I meant he's in London. I don't know what I'd do without him. He's the only one who can really get me away from all this and put it all into perspective. You know he never lets anyone talk about anything except himself.'

'Don't be mean about my brother. I'm sure he's a great help.'

'I can say anything I like about him. I mean, I know he's adorable and lovable and so good-looking I drool every time I see him, but I think describing him as a great help is probably a gross exaggeration.'

'Annabel! You're supposed to be in love with him.' Mimi didn't push the issue. She knew better than to fight with Annabel about affairs of the heart. 'When does your mother arrive?'

'Ugh. I think she's here already. She's probably making Kenneth rearrange all the flowers in her suite as we speak. Honestly, Mimi, I sometimes wonder whether it was worth taking all that money to set up the business from her. I've had to design a whole section of the collection for ageing beautiful people, just for her, and I know she's still going to try and make me give all the evening dresses sleeves so that she won't have to show her scraggy old woman's arms. All I can say is that she'd better buy the section I've designed for her or I'll shoot her with my handy kalashnikov and find new backers, and only design clothes for underage anorexics like everyone else.'

'Annabel, don't worry so much. London's so hot these days you could design a collection worthy of the Crimplene section of M&S and the international press would still rave about it. You English can do no wrong at the moment.'

'And exactly how much pride did you say had to come before a fall?'

Mimi sighed, exasperated. 'And are you casted?'

'Yes, Mimi.'

'You didn't give in to that girl who was just a bit too Salon Selectives for my liking?'

'No. There isn't one model who's got even the slightest bit of an adorable turned-up nose, freckles, naff hair or anything remotely obvious or twee. I couldn't afford any of those ones. All my lot have the right to look furious as they're doing it for free, Pandora included. Your mother would think they were all perfectly hideous – apart from Pandora. You'd have been impressed with my determination. Even the boys are delicious.'

'Boys?'

'Yes, boys. George decided we must have boys to accompany the girls. Frankly I think he's just desperately looking for a new boyfriend. He and Rory Williams – you know, Nina Charles' style director – took over the atelier the other day and spent the whole afternoon enthroned on our very expensive new armchairs having juniors from the atelier Polaroid a parade of beauties. Honestly, it was like Christmas, birthday and Easter rolled into one for both of them. I thought they were going to explode with excitement.'

'Duncan must have loved it.'

'Yeah, right. I don't think he even noticed. He's so worried about justifying everything to my mother tomorrow.'

'Poor thing.'

'Well, it is his job.'

'Still, your mother's quite an ogre. To deal with her first thing in the morning's enough to terrify anybody.'

'So?'

Mimi gave up and changed the subject. 'So – it will be a success if Rory's behind you. I mean, he is the only man capable of making opinions in the UK overnight.'

'Behind George, you mean. He took him out to a razzy dinner afterwards. He can't have liked any of the boys they Polaroided that much if he could only find my lovely little assistant to take out afterwards. Besides, you know him – any excuse not to go to his office. And as for me, sometimes I'm just too nice for my own good. I've got to learn to do things for myself, not let people bulldoze me into letting them take the limelight when I'm the one taking all the creative risks.'

'Do the boys work?'

'Thanks for the pep talk. Yes, they do.'

'Good. Right. Stop whingeing then and go to bed, Annabel. I'll see you tomorrow.'

'I'm not whingeing!'

'Bed . . .'

'Put it there.'

'Here?'

'No, there, you stupid boy. Honestly, anybody would think you were a halfwit from the little you understand of what I say.'

Kenneth French slammed down a huge arrangement of white lilac on the marble-topped side table in his mother's sitting room and turned on her. Tiny, blond and with a bee-stung pout modelled on years of examining Brigitte Bardot movies, his ice-blue eyes glinted with fury and his fists were clenched in frustration.

'Not only is that unkind, Mother, but it's not politically correct to make vicious comments about people's mental abilities. One of these days you'll regret spending all your life telling people they're stupid.'

'You darling, you. People, on the whole, are relatively intelligent. You, on the other hand, are not the most gifted man in the brains department and I do wish you'd realise it.' Oonagh French sat down unnecessarily heavily on a yellow silk sofa in her suite at Blakes, changed her mind and moved to a purple velvet armchair which went better with her suit, and sighed with exhaustion. 'I've got jet lag,' she announced. 'Where's Gladstone?'

'Mother, it's hard enough for me to keep track of your flower arrangements. Besides, if I'm so dumb how can I be expected to know anything about the movements of your lover? And you can't have jet lag when you've only taken a train.'

'Don't be bitchy tonight, darling. Come on, let's order dinner. It'll make us feel better until our respective lovers turn up.'

'Not hungry. And you shouldn't be either. You'll burst one of these days, Mother.'

Oonagh smoothed the duck-egg blue, spring weight, bouclé, Dior couture suit she was wearing over her size eight hips and shook out her expensively dyed blonde shoulder-length mane. It was the bane of her life that her children had inherited their father's platinum hair and that she was forced to pretend that she hadn't been born with hair of such a dull colour that she couldn't quite even remember what it was.

'I don't know how you can be so cruel to your own mother. Talk about making personal comments! Gladstone loves my curves.'

'It's easy, Mother. You just ask for it.' Kenneth snapped open the curtains and stared moodily down at the street below.

The door slammed open.

'It's OK. Everyone can relax now. I am 'ere.' A tiny bomb of a man burst into the room and did a rather contrived puckish dance over to Oonagh, upon whom he breathed rather than kissed, and then to Kenneth who threw his arms around the newcomer, his face lit up with delight.

'Jean-Luc, where've you been? I've been worried sick about you and all this time I've been stuck on my own with the neighbourhood beached whale and nobody else to talk to.'

'Oh, my precious little darling!' the French bomb screeched, his bobbed peroxided hair bouncing up and down with enthusiasm. 'You mean you really missed me? Oh, I sink I will cry wizz ze emotion.' He collapsed onto a chair, carefully pulling the tails of his purple velvet Gucci jacket down before his arse hit the upholstery. Drama was one thing but there was no need to ruin one's clothes in the process. 'Oh, sweetheart. Isn't it lovely to be in London? I brought really no luggage so we 'ave to shop like mad sings tomorrow or I will 'ave absolutely nossing to wear to your sister's little événement.'

Kenneth looked over at his mother, nervously tucking the ends of his immaculate naturally blond Little Lord Fauntleroy bob over his ears. 'Jean-Luc, how could you? You know I've spent all this month's allowance. Now we'll have to be lovely to Mummy or we won't even be able to get into Marks and Sparks, let alone that lovely Ozwald Boateng in Savile Row.'

'Oh dear. 'Ave you two been squabbling again? 'Ow is it zat Gladstone and I can never leave you alone for more zan five minutes before you fight again? Really, you both need to grow up.'

'Gladstone.' Oonagh stamped her foot. 'Where is he? He should've been here hours ago.'

'Relax, Oonagh darling. 'E was on ze train wizz me. I sink he went quickly somewhere and zen 'e will come 'ere. Some very odd story about looking for a beet of work. Bah, what will he sink of next?'

Neither Oonagh nor Kenneth took any notice of the threat of Gladstone actually trying to earn a living. Kenneth just thought Jean-Luc's French accent was adorable and Oonagh was swept away by the thought that in a matter of minutes her ghastly son and his horrible boyfriend would be banished from her suite by her masterful lover who would then take her in his arms and tell her that he wanted to cover her in paint and bathe in her. She shivered in anticipation.

Annabel rolled off Antonio, pushing her hair out of her eyes. She leaned forward and smoothed away the beads of sweat that glistened on his forehead, then kissed his drowsy eyes before reaching for his cigarettes and lighting him one, putting it directly between his lips. Antonio Ytuarte lay back on Annabel's bed and drew deeply on his Gauloise Blonde, accepting her attentions with a nonchalance she adored. Catching her breath she sat up, cross-legged, facing him and watched him exhale. The smoke blended against the shining silver walls, inspired by the Duchesse de Noailles.

Annabel's flat was created as a homage to French 1920s interior design, all glossy veneer and orange velvet. She had no time for minimalist white, however fashionable it was. She'd spent a fortune as well as a great deal of time finding the perfect pieces of furniture in the grander parts of the Parisian flea markets and the specialist shops in the Rue de Seine. She loved her apartment and Antonio complemented it perfectly. He was so gorgeous to look at that sometimes she wished he would lie absolutely still for hours so that she could just drink in the sight of him. He was the only person who could take her mind off her forthcoming show. His jet-black hair was oiled back from his strong-featured face, his stomach was taut and rippling, his legs were long and muscular, his shoulders . . . She sighed. No, even he couldn't take her mind off her work tonight. She longed for the show to be over. She'd had enough of this collection. After the show she'd give anything to never have to see the clothes again. But in reality she'd have to make a round-the-world trip with all her clothes to sell them, to cover her costs, to repay her mother, to please Duncan . . . What was wrong with it? Pandora swinging in the dévoré flashed through her mind.

Antonio's deep, slightly accented Argentinian voice woke her from her dream. She jumped.

'What are you groaning for, my little Annabel? Is it the thought that I might make love to you again tonight?'

She smiled and stretched out on her stomach along the end of the bed. At least he was trying to take her mind off things. She waited for his expert hands to reach for her, and when they didn't she put her tear ducts to work to no great effect before she resigned herself to his leaving.

'I've got to go. Big meeting tomorrow. I need my beauty sleep, and you know how bad I am at sleeping when I share a bed.'

'Can't you stay a little while?' she sniffed tearfully. He was already in the shower.

'Sorry, darling. You'll be all right. Take one of those pills the doctor gave you. You look tired, little one. Get some sleep tonight and then tomorrow I promise . . .' He grinned at her through the bathroom door, one eyebrow raised suggestively.

'I can't see you then, Antonio. It's the show the day after tomorrow – I'll be in the atelier all night.'

'Oh, this stupid show.' He came towards her, wrapped only in a tiny towel, and put his arms around her. 'I wish you'd never got involved in this company. I don't like sharing you with all those people. I want you to be all mine, in a cosy nest, with me for ever.'

'I know, Antonio. But you do understand, don't you?' Annabel blinked back her tears prettily. 'I can't live off Mummy for the rest of my life, can I?'

'If only I could keep you myself. One day I will have my own multinational corporation and you'll have no excuse to do anything but be there for me. I can't bear it that you want more. I simply don't understand why a millionaire should try to earn another living when they're already going to inherit a fortune . . .'

'Unless Mother spends it all on Gladstone first,' Annabel interrupted, her tears suddenly drying up.

'Unlikely but possible.' Antonio laughed. 'Well, in spite of that I'll try to understand and I'll leave you to get on with your little show.' He kissed her on the nose. 'I'll see you afterwards, baby, OK?'

'But you will be there?'

'Of course. With Mimi in town I can hardly not turn up. You'd understand but she'd have my guts for garters.' Dressed in black jeans, Gucci loafers, a white T-shirt and Cutler and Gross sunglasses in spite of the fact that it was one in the morning, he slung his jacket over his shoulder, kissed her hard on the lips and headed towards the door.

'*Ciao, bella.*'

'*Ciao.*' Annabel lazily lit one of Antonio's cigarettes and began to play back her collection in her head, searching in vain for the missing link which was driving her mad.

George sat on the night bus from Ludgate Circus. He'd waited nearly an hour for it to arrive, shivering and grumbling to himself. 'All I need is enough money to cab it home if I work till after midnight. Is that too much to ask?' he said aloud. A girl sitting across the aisle from him got up and moved. Night buses were always full of mad men, and this one with his five o'clock stubble, a kirby grip, grubby overcoat and bright pink jeans looked weirder than most. 'Talk to Duncan,' George told himself. 'Talk to Duncan – he'll persuade her to be nicer to me.' He leaned back and replayed in his mind the pictures of Pandora dancing in the dévoré. Drifting into a pleasant doze, he missed his stop at Camberwell Green and woke up at Dulwich Plough. After he had walked back to his house, he hardly had time to iron a clean shirt, shave and eat toast before he had to go back to the atelier.

Gladstone Frith, five foot six of pure power wrapped in purply-chocolate skin, was late. He knew that Oonagh would be making Jean-Luc and Kenneth's lives miserable but he had an errand to run which couldn't wait. Darker in his black Comme des Garçons suit and silent in No Name sneakers, he consulted his gold Rolex, then slipped down Curzon Street, avoiding street lights, and headed into the tiny maze of Shepherd Market. No one except Duncan saw him, and Duncan hardly noticed the shadowy figure who rang a bell across the street beside the Lebanese restaurant. Duncan was staring out of the window of his little Shepherd Market flat, a plate of untouched scrambled eggs and a half empty glass of port on the little table by his chair. His attempt to read himself to sleep had failed, and his battered copy of *The Brothers Karamazov* lay abandoned on his lap.

It was only when the door opposite didn't open as speedily as it usually did to admit the stranger that

Duncan took note. He shut *The Brothers Karamazov* and stared blindly at the dark figure by the door on the other side of the street. Gladstone turned away, and for a moment his face was fully illuminated by the light from the sign above the restaurant and Duncan recognised him. Typical, he thought, not only is Oonagh a professional flake but the man she's supporting so passionately is spending all her money on tarts. The door opened, and Duncan caught a glimpse of carefully oiled hair. Surely it wasn't . . . He peered more closely. Yes, it was Antonio. The Argentinian slapped Gladstone on the back, then the door to the building shut behind the two men. So the lover of his business partner's mother was sharing prostitutes with his boss's boyfriend! What the hell was going on? Duncan prepared to wait until they left. Two hours later he was satisfied that at least Antonio and Gladstone were not planning on staying the night in his neighbourhood bordello.

'Where've you been?' Oonagh did the sulky little girl thing with her shoulders and her mouth that had worked in her youth when trapping her late husband, but was less successful now she was in her forties.

'Oonagh, Oonagh, please don't be cross. I had to see a dealer. He could only see me late but I showed him the little things I'd brought and he's interested. He might give me an exhibition.'

'In London?' Oonagh screeched and leapt to her feet to embrace Gladstone, her transparent white silk baby doll nightdress dancing out of time with her shrivelled little breasts. She didn't notice that he hadn't brought his portfolio with him and that therefore he was plainly lying. 'But darling, why didn't you tell me? I know everyone in London. I'm sure he knows me, and in that case of course he'll help.'

'It's early days, Oonagh, and anyway I long for you to be proud of me when I've achieved something on my own. I know how you like to help, but one of these days I've got to learn to stand on my own two feet.' He ran his hands through her hair, bending to kiss her neck. Oonagh was not so easily distracted. She slapped him away.

'Oh, don't be ridiculous. What's my money for if it's not for spending on you? And if you really loved me it would be enough that I know you're a genius and you wouldn't need the acknowledgement of the rest of the world.'

'But I want you to be proud of me, Oonagh.' He nibbled on an earlobe. Not a successful move. She pushed him away again.

'I am, precious, I am. Now, do you mind just checking on Kenneth and Jean-Luc for me? And then you can come and give me a teeny little massage and help me drink this yummy champagne that's been sweating in anticipation of your arrival in its little ice bucket here. Help me take away the stress of the journey.'

'Oonagh, why does Kenneth need checking on? He is an adult, you know.'

'I know, but please, darling, he sees you as such a

father figure he'd miss you if you didn't pop in to say good night.'

'This is ridiculous.'

'Don't be grouchy. Run along, darling, and I'll open the champagne.'

Gladstone headed for the door, struggling to hide his irritation. He flashed his pearly teeth at Oonagh and blew her a kiss. 'Don't move. We need to take up where we've left off – promise!'

'All right, my little chocolate button, but don't make Mummy wait too long,' she admonished.

Gladstone hurried down the corridor to Kenneth and Jean-Luc's suite. Champagne – he hated the stuff. He'd do anything for a beer. He wondered if there would ever be a limit to what he'd do for money? Knocking on the door and entering the war zone of Kenneth and Jean-Luc's room, he thought probably not.

Jean-Luc lounged in an armchair, feet on a pouf, large crystal glass almost empty of red wine hanging from one hand, a three quarters smoked Gitane in the other. He looked up and smiled leeringly at Gladstone.

'Fellow traveller. Good meeting?'

'Fine.' Gladstone leaned against the door jamb while Jean-Luc swigged the rest of his wine. 'Where's Kenneth?' Gladstone wasn't nervous. He sounded shifty because that was his nature, especially when confronted by Jean-Luc whom he trusted as much as he might any snake, poisonous or otherwise.

'In ze bass. Take a pew, why don't you?' Jean-Luc stood and went to find the decanter of wine on the drinks tray by the door.

'Gotta go. The old lady's waiting. If I'm here too long I expect she'll come and try and join in, and I'm sure that's the last thing you want. Besides, as you and Kenneth are obviously planning something extremely dodgy I'd hate to hang around and prevent you from discussing it further. Must leave you some time for your beauty sleep, mustn't I?'

'I couldn't care less. And as for Oonagh, she is an old lady – sooner or later she will die. Perhaps we should make ze most of her company while it lasts.'

'Don't be sick, Jean-Luc. Antonio and I'll get your little plan out of you sooner or later – but not tonight. I'm exhausted and I'm off. Night.'

'Ah, ze poor little lover boy. Go and do your little circus act for her – sing for your supper. I don't know how you can bear it.'

'You're in exactly the same game, Jean-Luc.'

'Rubbish! My baby's a beautiful boy – a little stupid perhaps, but you are doing circus tricks for a woman twice your age and for half ze rewards. If I were you I'd get shot of 'er, you know. Perhaps you should really try to earn a living. Some of ziss art you're always talking about. Why don't you prove yourself and sell some?'

'Fuck off, Jean-Luc! Go earn a living yourself if you think it's that much preferable to living with a boy you despise.'

'Shh, Gladstone! We don't need the cheque books to 'ear us, now do we?'

But Gladstone hadn't stayed to argue. He was already gone, slamming the door furiously behind him. Kenneth appeared from the shower, almost innocent-looking in his white towelling bathrobe and rumpled hair.

'Hello, my love.'

'Darling – drink?' Jean-Luc poured a glass for his lover. 'I was just talking to Gladstone who so kindly came to wish us good night. Oonagh let him out of his cage for half an hour. I reminded him zat your muzzer will not be 'ere forever. 'E seemed quite put out at ze idea.'

'Don't be morbid, Jean-Luc. I never took you for a voyeur. Are you going to relish this like some kind of serial killer or something?'

'Darling don't be silly. In my book murder is an art form and zerefore worth relishing as much as any little moment at ze Royal Academy.'

'What! You're not implying that I might actually enjoy going to Europe for a month of hotel rooms and air kissing?' Mimi Ytuarte pouted down the phone and twisted a jet-black curl behind her ear. She'd crashed into her apartment, thrown her armload of dry cleaning onto the sofa in her white sitting room, opened a bottle of Evian from the fridge and drunk half of it, then thrown herself down on her bed and reached for the phone. She needed to talk to her mother.

'Marianita, it's your job.' Her mother sounded as if her patience was running out.

'*Mamà*, don't call me Marianita. You know I hate it. And I know fashion's my job and I've spent most of my life so far trying to get into it, but I'll miss my apartment – I've only been here a week. The only person I really like seeing in Europe is Annabel, and she'll be all wrapped up in her collection – I'll never be able to see her on her own.'

'Well, she's going to be the big star if the next few weeks go well.'

'I know, and I'll just be her fat little friend who does all the supportive stuff.'

'You always wanted to work for a fashion magazine, and now you are I can't see what you're complaining about. What makes you suddenly long to be a star?'

'Nothing. I just know I'll spend all my time following Annabel around being helpful and we won't have one serious conversation during the time I'm with her.'

'So save the serious words till your holiday here in the summer. And you'll have many more cats to whip than just following Annabel around the place, won't you?'

Mimi sighed deeply. 'It's fish to fry in English, *Mamà*. I'm so junior they're making me go to all those terrible shows that the designers have to virtually pay people to go to, and I'll only have standing places behind the pillars at anything worth seeing.'

'Except at Annabel's.'

'Yes. Well, I'm having a tough time persuading the editor in chief to go to that, and the magazine's even refusing to photograph the runway for the files. It's not fair. Just because Annabel's new.'

'You'll just have to make them see how brilliant she is, then. You'll have to photograph it yourself, won't you?'

'I've sorted that already. There's a friend of mine who seems to be photographing every single show in the vain hope that someone will want the pictures, so I'll make his day and buy Annabel's from him. I've just been telling Annabel that the Brits can't put a foot wrong, but it's not quite true. My editor in chief's English and she couldn't care less about recently graduated fashion designers who haven't been blooded on the minefield of international luxury sales before. The fact that my boss is also a prize bitch has very little to do with it.'

'Already you're being brilliant. You must be careful with your manipulation skills, Mimi. One day you'll turn into a creeper.'

'The expression's come a cropper, *Mamà*.'

'Whatever. In any case, you'll see. Nothing's too difficult.'

'No . . . But you're changing the subject. Imagine, *Mamà* – a month of aeroplanes and crappy hotels which I'm forced to stay in because I'm not grand enough to stay in the posh ones on expenses.'

'Stop complaining. You love all this. I know you do. You can't wait to have to elbow your way to the front of queues and fight for your place and drink too much champagne at promotional parties and stay up late with Annabel gossiping about everyone else's terrible taste.'

'Oh, let me complain, *Mamà*.'

'Only because I'm the only person who'll let you get away with it. Annabel would have stopped all this by now. Frankly, darling, I can't see why you don't pay for your own hotels and then you could have your usual rooms in all these cities. And then at least you'd be rested when you have to endure all this elbowing through crowds that I know you enjoy so much.'

'It's very simple. I can't pay my own way because I'm working, *Mamà*. At least in London I can stay with Antonio, but everywhere else it's going to third-rate hotels. Imagine how Gloria Wharton would feel if she found her room at the Ritz in Paris had been given to me because I've been a client there all my life and she's just a jumped-up little tart who's only been editor in chief of the magazine I scurry about for for a mere eight months and isn't likely to last in her job through the next four weeks. I'd be fired quicker than a quick thing.'

'I wish you'd stop whining. It won't be that bad. What about Annabel's business partner? I thought you said he would be worth going round the world a hundred times for, if only to catch a glimpse of him.'

'God, *Mamà* . . .'

'Don't blaspheme.'

'Sorry. Well, he is gorgeous. I don't understand why Annabel doesn't see it.'

'Perhaps because he isn't compared to your brother.'

'I suppose so. But you could hardly call Antonio a reliable character. When I met Duncan . . . He might not have those rather obvious South American looks, but he's so sure of himself. Imagine – an accountant! I'd never have to worry about paying my bills again.'

'You don't now. Besides, he isn't a Catholic, is he?'

'So?'

'Well, don't get too carried away – your father would die if you married out of the faith.'

'Don't be ridiculous. He's been having affairs with every available maid and stable girl ever since he was born. His faith lies in the power of his swarthy looks to catch anything passing in a skirt or beautifully cut jodh-purs.'

'But that didn't make him marry unsuitably, did it?'

'I don't know how you put up with it, *Mamà*. And anyway, Annabel isn't Catholic. You don't mind that.'

'She's chic enough to get away with it. Besides, you can't marry an accountant – they're inevitably boring.'

'Duncan's not boring. He has hidden depths. I'm sure of it.'

'I don't believe it to be possible. How's the packing?'

'Terrible.'

Mimi's bedroom was a disaster zone: piles of clothes were strewn around in no sort of order and certainly in no state to be put into her matching Louis Vuitton luggage with the gold initials which she'd been given for her twenty-first birthday. Ten years of boarding school should have given her at least a talent for packing, but she had no more idea how to follow the travel tips given in the mag-azine she worked for than Oonagh did.

'Well, you'd better start soon. You know how bad you are at it. When's your flight?'

'Tomorrow morning at eleven.'

'And they're making you fly steerage?'

'Yes. But I'll be upgraded.'

'But not Concorde?'

'No, *Mamà*, and I'm not about to put myself on it, because the other editors will be cross. They've had to work for their Concorde tickets. I'd be banned from all the parties for being flash if I paid my own flight.'

'Honestly, darling, why don't I order you a hair shirt for your birthday? I didn't realise this job was going to be a punishment for your father having given you so much.'

'I'll live, *Mamà*.' And then, in a little voice, 'I wish you were coming.'

'I know, darling, but I can't. Your father hates it when I'm away – and you'll be here in the summer with Annabel and Antonio and that terrible Kenneth. It's not long till then. And imagine – we'll have so much to catch up on, it'll be wonderful.'

'I love you, *Mamà*.'

'I love you too, darling. Now, pack quickly and go to bed and get some sleep. It sounds as if you'll need it with all this flying around in the back of aeroplanes and sleeping in nasty little hotels.'

Mimi went to bed and slept like a dark-haired angel, having only packed a brand-new Prada party dress and some face cream and a couple of pairs of knickers. She'd have to nip to Michaeljohn in London to have her bits waxed tomorrow, in case she ever got within kissing distance of Duncan. She couldn't bear to not be prepared for that eventuality.

Chapter 2

Six am. It was still dark and Annabel had the atelier to herself. She made herself a steaming expresso using tokens for the machine stolen from Duncan's drawer, and collected the diary she'd been keeping during her work on her first collection. She perched on a stool by one of the huge cutting tables and opened the diary at the first page. Only then did she look at the collection. She liked what she saw. Yes, she'd stayed true to the spirit of her inspiration: the lines were clean; the colours were simple, muted even. She stared long and hard at the belted suits, the tailored pants, the businesslike shirts, the shiny leather belts, and then waited patiently for her persistent eye to tell her where the collection failed to be absolutely perfect. And slowly, the idea stumbling forward from somewhere in her subconscious, she realised where the weak link lay. The lines were *too* clean. The neat cleverness of each piece would be lost with nothing to put it into perspective.

Back in her studio she hunted about until she found a box she'd discarded at the beginning of her work, containing wild silk roses, feather boas, long strings of pearls and velvet ribbons. Very gently, careful not to go over the top, she began to decorate the models – a pink rose at the belt of a khaki felt suit, a strip of dark red velvet in the buttonhole of a lapel, a string of pearls around the cuff of Pandora's long-sleeved dove-grey dévoré evening dress. And to her relief the collection came to life.

Two hours later she sat back on her heels, a glow of exertion colouring the previously grey planes of her face. She was almost satisfied. The atelier staff were going to have to work flat out to make enough roses and ribbon finishings to satisfy the whole collection, but it would be marvellous, a sign of flippancy, of devil may care for the dark days preceding the spring.

Upside down, pinning the last rose to the hem of a dark chocolate mousseline Edwardian-inspired tea dress, she didn't hear Duncan arrive.

He gave her a friendly pat on her backside. 'Here already?'

She jumped, blushing furiously. 'Duncan! You might have warned me.'

Dressed in an ancient and rather crumpled tweed jacket with cracked leather patches on the elbows, a pale pink double-cuffed New and Lingwood shirt, crisply ironed by his cleaning lady, and worn 501s, none of which Annabel noticed, his eyes swept over the rejuvenated collection. 'It's wonderful. Much better.'

'Thanks.'

'I mean – not that I know anything about this sort of stuff, but it's beautiful.'

'I just hope the atelier are going to be able to magic enough of these up in time.'

'I'm sure you'll whip them into shape. I'll help if I can.' He picked up a rose and looked at it thoughtfully. 'On second thoughts, perhaps I'd better leave it to the experts. I failed at cutting and gluing at kindergarten. I'd probably ruin everything for you.'

'Do you want some coffee?' Annabel was already halfway to the expresso machine at the end of the atelier, rooting around in her pockets for more stolen tokens. Without thinking she gave them to Duncan and he took them; naturally he would make coffee for her, even though the thought of coffee for himself made him feel physically sick.

'No thanks. I'm wound up enough already. My stomach's got enough acid in it to make a really dangerous industrial cleaner.'

'Never mind. I'm sure you'll be fine. My mother may be a dragon but I know you'll make a valiant St George.'

'Hmm . . . I hope so. Just so long as you don't spend too much on all these roses, no more overtime for anybody, and promise me you'll sell a half a million's worth next week, and we'll be fine.'

Annabel laughed. 'I'll do anything to avoid running to Mummy.'

'Is she here yet?'

'Should have arrived last night. She'll probably turn up

here in a minute and expect us all to buzz around her like bees. Perhaps I can get some sedative I can inject her with until all this is over.'

'If only you could persuade Gladstone to keep her away from us.'

'Chance'd be a fine thing. He'll just sit there and do as he's told, as usual. Spineless fool.'

'I didn't think he was such mates with Antonio though. Sugar?'

Annabel nodded. 'Antonio?'

Duncan added the two heaped spoonfuls he knew perfectly well she took in her coffee, and handed the cup to her. 'I saw them together last night.'

'No, you can't have. Antonio was with me and then he went home to bed. You're imagining things, Duncan.'

'Maybe.' Duncan turned towards his office, squaring his shoulders.

'Once more unto the breach, dear friend, once more.'

Annabel laughed and Duncan grinned grimly as he shut his door behind him. It was no comfort to him that it didn't look as though Annabel had slept at all either. He wasn't going to cause trouble by describing in detail where and in what circumstances he'd spied Antonio the night before.

Annabel perched on the end of the table, waiting for the first members of the atelier staff to arrive and wishing George was there to amuse her. She sipped her coffee. Antonio had already gone from her mind.

*

'Mother, please!'

'No.'

'Why not?'

'Because you're a stupid little boy and you should have made Jean-Luc pack more efficiently.'

'That's not a reason. I'm *not* stupid!'

'You sound like a six-year-old.'

'Only because you only ever listen to me when I pretend to be a child.'

'Don't be petulant.'

'I'm not. But I need a little bit of money. Otherwise Jean-Luc and I are just going to have to go everywhere with you today, and I know you've got all those desperately important business meetings with the Incredible Hulk at Annabel's office, and you really don't want me there to ruin your professional businesswoman look.'

Oonagh examined herself critically in the mirror. Jill Sander pinstriped suit, the jacket slung over her shoulders, triple-ply Chanel cashmere beneath, Ralph Lauren overcoat with lovely masterful army shoulders. Kenneth did have a point. If he came along he would ruin the line. She sipped at the coffee on the tray beside her.

'*Please*, Mummy.'

'Oh, you are the most irritating little child.'

Kenneth knew he'd won. There was no need to speak. He held his breath as she reached for her bag. It was too far away.

'Oh, darling – you can take a card. Just promise me not to go too over the top and don't ask me for the pin number. You'll only spend thousands of pounds on useless things if I do that. And tell Jean-Luc that purple velvet does nothing for his hair. If you must spend money on him, why don't you take him to Savile Row and have a little party at Gieves and Hawkes on your father's old account? It's still open, you know. He'd look much better in grey. And not so fitted.'

'Savile Row it is, Mother.' Kenneth did a little dance round the credit card. Ha, ha. He had no intention of telling her he was planning on going berserk at Ozwald Boateng across the road from Gieves and Hawkes. If it was Savile Row she wanted then Savile Row she would get.

Gloria Wharton, editor in chief of the biggest and glossiest fashion magazine in the world, stepped off Concorde spitting tacks. That irritating little editor Mimi was just going to have to go. She couldn't bear it that the girl paid her own Concorde tickets. She wasn't to know that Mimi was such a valued customer of British Airways that she was automatically upgraded to Concorde whenever she could catch the flight. Mimi hadn't realised this either but had been secretly thrilled when a car turned up on her Manhattan doorstep that morning to pick her up. Fortunately she'd only managed to pack an overnight bag the night before so she only had a holdall to carry and the inevitable bottle of Evian. Gloria didn't even know how many pieces of luggage she had and could hardly manage them. And she certainly wasn't going to have this little

South American upstart help her with them. Someone might see them and think they were friends!

Mimi carefully maintained a respectful distance behind Gloria as they made their way through Terminal 4 and achieved another faux pas in being grabbed by Nina Charles, Gloria's arch rival at the group's English magazine, who kissed her hello in front of a handy batch of paparazzi and offered her a lift in her silver BMW Z3 which was waiting at the kerb. Not only was Gloria's car just a black limo, but her useless assistant had got the time wrong, so she had to wait and watch while Mimi threw her bag into the back of Nina's car and helped Nina put the roof down to make the most of the fabulous March sunshine. Mimi wrapped her vintage Gucci faux Mongolian lamb jacket tightly round herself, then jumped into the passenger seat and sped off into the traffic laughing with Nina. Gloria was left alone, unattended and surrounded by too much not-quite-matching luggage. Since starting her new job, she hadn't had time to sort out her bag situation, and her Hervé Chapeliers were a little bit ragged at the corners. She stamped her foot and started making notes in the huge Hermès day diary she kept with her at all times, not even noticing her hefty, over-the-top car when it arrived.

'I didn't see you on the plane, Mimi. You look marvellous.'

'Oh Nina, you are sweet.' Mimi giggled. 'I look ten kilos overweight but I can't lose it because I'm too fond of my tits.'

Nina laughed. 'You're lovely just as you are. I wish I had a bit more shape.'

'Don't – you have the most perfect body in fashion.'

'It's just a foot too short.'

'Good for elbowing your way through crowds. Not that you have to do much of that. Are you coming to Annabel's show?'

'Of course, darling. Her leaving show at St Martin's was a huge event. I can't wait to see what she's come up with. I expect you know all about it.'

'Yes. But I'm sworn to secrecy.'

'Of course you are. Where's she showing?'

'Aha . . .'

'All right – I'll have to wait till tomorrow. Do you think the invitations self-destruct minutes after opening them in order to prevent hoi polloi like Gloria finding out about the venue?'

'Gloria couldn't care less. She's refusing even to photograph it. I'm so glad you're coming.'

'I wouldn't miss it for the world. Gloria's a bigger fool than I thought she was. It'll be the talk of the season, you wait, and she won't even have been there. Honestly, since she's moved to the States her head's got so big I'm surprised they allow her on Concorde. Surely swelling heads are bad for pressurised cabins? She can't have liked you being on it much.'

'No. And unfortunately we were put next to each other. I had to pretend I didn't know that she'd taken my window seat. And she hardly stayed sitting the whole way over. I had to keep my knees in the aisle all the time so she could get back and forth.'

As they cruised into London Mimi quizzed Nina about her London friends.

'How's Pandora?'

'Fine, her usual self – still fighting with Rory over the suitability of their various boyfriends and still rising inexorably to the top of her profession. She's doing Annabel's show, though, which is kind of her. Annabel isn't paying.'

'I know. But Pandora hardly needs the money any more, does she? At least, not since you gave her that cover with Morgan James in Morocco last year. She's been so in demand that I should think she only gets to sleep on long-haul flights.'

'No, but she could have got bigheaded. You know her.'

'And what about you, now you've settled down into married bliss with your hunky architect?' Mimi sighed. 'Sam McAllistair . . . You know, the whole of the West Coast went into mourning when he moved over to the UK to be with you. How about some babies?'

Nina blushed and laughed out loud to cover her embarrassment. 'I'm a bit old for that.'

'Don't be ridiculous. In New York fashion people buy children in bulk like accessories. I slightly wonder if they get them on sale or return so they can send them back if they don't suit.'

The car headed towards the Hammersmith flyover.

'Where are you staying?'

'With Antonio. The magazine were going to put me in

such a disgusting hotel and I can't possibly pay for my own room at Blakes – Gloria really would kill me then – so I've taken the lesser of two evils.'

'Well, at least his apartment's so huge you'll only have to see each other if you plan it.'

'I know. And I can make sure he goes to Annabel's show. You know what he's like. He's liable to wriggle out of it if he's worked out that all the attention will be on Annabel and none on him.'

'What does Annabel see in him?'

'She fancies him so rotten she can't see past the muscles.'

'Poor girl. She's such a sweet thing, I can't bear to see her trampled on like that. She's no fool. I can't understand why she doesn't see it.'

'Well, they say love is blind and they're wrong – in this case it's everything but blind. I suppose it keeps him out of trouble a bit, her keeping an eye on him. I feel less responsible for him.'

'Not much you could do from New York anyway.'

'I know. But you know how my mother worries. If it wasn't for Annabel I might have taken the job you offered me.'

'I wish you had. I've never really replaced Gloria and I think you might have trained up to be a senior stylist very nicely. I still don't understand why you went to New York. Working so closely with Gloria and Don must be terrible.'

'Understatement of the century. Everything that's rotten in magazine publishing's concentrated within twenty feet of my office. Still, at least from Manhattan it's easier to get to Argentina. And what a learning curve! If I can survive this and still make a place for myself in the fashion industry then I'll be made for life. After all, Gloria and Don on a CV may not mean I did anything particularly brilliant but at least it proves I'm resilient.'

Nina laughed. 'That's like saying that banging your head against a brick wall's good because you appreciate it when you stop.' She drew up at the next traffic lights. 'Where does the terrible Antonio live?'

'Royal Avenue.'

'Just next door to me. I'll drop you right there.'

'Thanks, Nina. I'm so glad you were there – even if it did make Gloria spit.'

'I'm glad especially because it made Gloria spit.'

Annabel jumped a mile high as the atelier door slammed open behind her. She turned to find her mother and Gladstone striking a pose in the doorway and waiting while the whole company turned to stare.

'Mother.'

'Daaaarrrrling!' Oonagh growled and marched forward, discarding her coat on the floor for Gladstone to gather up and deal with. She hugged her daughter carefully in order to avoid crushing her 'look'.

'How nice to see you.' Annabel hated the way she spoke to her mother; a mixture of guilty little girl and bored acolyte. 'Gladstone.' She shook his hand. She loathed him so much there was no way she was going to kiss him. He loathed her in return. After all, she'd only recently cost her mother two million pounds in investment which Oonagh could perfectly well have spent on him. Duncan appeared from his office, trying to calm his hair which he'd been tearing at since he'd arrived that morning and wiping his glasses on his tie.

'Mrs French.' He went to shake Oonagh's hand but she grabbed him in a bear hug.

'Darling – have you been looking after my precious little Annabel? My goodness, you both look tired.' She opened her arms wide in a gesture of largesse. 'Let me take you both out to lunch to give you a little break, yes?'

'Mother, I can't. I'm sorry. I've got so much to do.'

'You can't be so swamped you haven't got time to see your own financial backer.' Oonagh laughed in astonishment.

'Mrs French, please.' Duncan ushered her towards his office, frightened that Annabel might be going to burst into tears. 'May I take you through a few things first? I'm very keen to show you where we are and how our projections are coming on for the next season.'

Oonagh tried not to look too bored at the prospect. 'Come along, Gladstone. You can help explain the bits I don't understand.'

But Gladstone was having none of this. Having delivered his mistress into the arms of her daughter, he had no intention of sticking around. Squaring shoulders that would have impressed Genghis Khan, he turned to oil his way out of this potentially sticky situation. 'Oonagh, precious. Please, let me go. It's such ages since I've been in London. Excuse me while I go and soak up the atmosphere. I've missed it.' He kissed her behind her ear. 'And you know how I need to be alone sometimes.'

'Oh, the artistic spirit. Of course you must go and nurture your soul.' Everyone in the atelier winced. As if the man had a soul to nurture! 'You know, he's looking for inspiration for a very big opening of his own in London.' Oonagh's gaze swept the assembled company. 'You'll all have to come and support him in exactly the same way we are supporting you.'

As Gladstone scuttled away Duncan wondered if he thought Oonagh's lover furtive only since he'd seen him the night before in Shepherd Market. He decided he was imagining things. He turned, smiled with all the charm he could muster at his employer's mother and ushered her into his office, closing the door behind him. At least he could help Annabel by letting her get on in peace.

Annabel turned back to her collection, rubbing her eyes and trying to regain her concentration. George looked up at her expectantly.

'And?' he asked.

'And what?' She'd lost it.

'Do you really want to re-hash all the evening dresses in the colours of the roses and put the roses on in moss green?'

'Yes. You'll have to use up that pink lining material we got for the army greatcoats, but I think it'll work. Just to have some colour. Otherwise everyone's going to leave

the show in tears. It'll look like a funeral. And everything's so pink already this season, I don't think I'll get
away with ignoring it totally.'

George, self-conscious, smoothed the old white jeans
he'd dyed fuchsia only a week ago. 'But the lining material's too stiff.'

'No it isn't. Watch.' Annabel grabbed a roll of pale wild
rose pink and cut a swathe. In a few swift movements the
fabric was pinned on a mannequin, a one-shouldered
bustier dress, an asymmetric hem – the dress would look
like a slash across a slim body. Oonagh certainly wouldn't
be able to get away with it. Much too much skin would be
on show. 'Get Gavin to rev that up into a dress. We can
have three of them – use the other red lining fabric and
then the fuchsia, they'll finish the whole thing off bril-
liantly. But we'll still finale with the dove-grey dévoré
evening dresses. Don't want to confuse the audience too
much.'

George stood back in amazement.

'Done.'

Gladstone jumped in a cab and went straight to visit
Antonio – his one and only real friend.

'Hi. Coffee? I've just made some.'

'Thanks.'

Antonio led the way down the long corridor of his
apartment in Royal Avenue towards his gleaming white
and black kitchen. Gladstone shivered. For a South
American Antonio had a curious aversion to central

heating. Or perhaps the chill of the apartment came from the fact that it was decorated in a manner reminiscent of the interior of a freezer. It was about as uncomfortable too.

'Everyone safely ensconced at Blakes then?'

'So far. I visited our little friends last night as you suggested.'

'And?'

'No clues. They're up to something, though. I've never seen Jean-Luc look so shifty. He positively glowed with nervous energy, and – lets face it – that's not something usually inspired by Kenneth.'

'Yeah. Kenneth's so dumb he can only inspire sleeping sickness in most people. I'm amazed Jean-Luc managed to look shiftier than he usually does.'

'Shiftier than a shifty thing, that one. And as for Kenneth, I didn't see him because he was bathing. And this morning I missed him. Oonagh made me do one of my party pieces last night – she always gets horny when she travels. I'm shattered. So I missed the son and heir this morning.'

'We'll get it out of them. And then we'll blackmail them in return for our silence.'

'It'll give us something to do while this fashion thing goes on. You know, there's a whole month of it. It's enough to make me go to Paris, make the most of the peace and quiet and actually paint.'

'Don't be ridiculous.'

'They'll tell us what they're up to. Kenneth always likes

an audience, and an audience of three is a dramatic improvement on just Jean-Luc.'

With exaggerated fastidiousness Antonio arranged coffee cups and coffee and a small box of very dark French chocolates onto a Fornasetti tray and led the way back to his white drawing room. He poured for them both, then lit a Gauloise, blowing smoke across his glass coffee table top directly at Gladstone's face. Gladstone coughed.

'Meanwhile I'm going to marry Annabel,' Antonio said confidently.

'If she'll have you.'

'She will.'

'Look, you go ahead and marry Annabel if you must, but that won't stop Oonagh pouring millions of dollars down the drain into Annabel's business. I mean, it's not as if she'll be successful, is it? The money will just disappear and you will be married to a declared bankrupt with no recourse to any money of your own. It's not as if your father'll give you any, is it? Or had you been planning to actually earn a living?' Antonio shifted uncomfortably on the sofa. 'No, of course not,' Gladstone said. 'Do you know how much she's put into Annabel's business?'

'No.'

'Do you have any idea? I mean, it's not as if Annabel has any business training, is it? A nice turn with pastel shades and a number of copycat party dresses is hardly going to pay back Mummy in a matter of minutes. On the contrary, I suspect that Mummy's going to be bankrupt herself before Annabel has finished pouring all the cash down the drain.'

'Yeah, well . . . The money's not going to run out this year, is it? I'm going to need a new car this summer, and my polo gear needs renovating, let alone the ponies in Berkshire. There'd better be money to pay for them . . .' Antonio looked meaningfully at his friend.

'We'd better get in there quickly before there's none left,' Gladstone said. 'I wonder what Oonagh's really worth.'

'If you're anything to go by, about three pounds fifty. More coffee, vicar?' Antonio poured.

Mimi stood waiting for Antonio to answer the doorbell. By the time she finally got into his flat she was fuming.

'Thanks for making me stand on the doorstep for hours. How charming you are, big brother.'

'Mimi, darling.' He hugged her and she dutifully kissed him hello.

'Have you any idea what kind of temperature it is out there?'

'It's a beautiful day. I hope you're wearing sun cream.'

'Don't be ridiculous. And it's freezing in here too. Can't you afford to put the heating on?' Mimi bustled along the passage to the spare room and dumped her bag on the bed. 'Right.' She marched back and surveyed Antonio's drawing room with distaste. 'Hi, Gladstone. Glad to see you two are already getting together. What little plans are you hatching today?'

'We're not hatching anything, just catching up. You look great, Mimi.'

'Hands off, Gladstone. You're bought and paid for, remember?' Mimi stepped smartly out of Gladstone's reach as he came forward to kiss her. 'I've got to go and see Annabel,' she said, reaching for her bamboo-handled black grosgrain Gucci holdall.

'I think I'll come with you.' Antonio grabbed his Armani black leather jacket and ushered her towards the door. 'Come on, Gladstone. Come and do your job.'

'No chance. I've got out of her clutches for a whole day. Do you have to go, Antonio? We could go and get some lunch.'

'I've got work to do, and that includes being nice to my girlfriend for five minutes.'

Gladstone laughed. 'What – you're going to propose now?'

''Course not. And for God's sake don't you say anything, Mimi – it's a surprise.'

'Hmm . . . you're really going to ask her to marry you?'

'Well, I've got to do it sooner or later. If I do it now then you'll have plenty of time to argue about wedding dresses before June.'

'June?'

'When we get married.'

'Glad you're so confident. What if she turns you down?' Mimi asked.

'She won't.'

'You're right. She thinks the sun shines out of your arse.'

'You put it so nicely, Mimi. Come on then, let's go.

Sorry, Gladstone, have to cut our little meeting short, I'm afraid.'

'That's OK. I'll go and pick up a film star or two at the Metropolitan bar.'

'Let's get out of here, Antonio.' Mimi led the way out of the apartment.

Antonio fastened his seatbelt in his convertible Audi coupé then turned to his sister.

'Now, which way is it to the atelier?'

'You mean you don't know?' Mimi was stunned

'Well, I don't exactly go there every day. Annabel has been working, you know. She hardly needs me around to distract her.' The car pulled out and rounded the corner into Radnor Walk.

'That way.' Mimi pointed down to the other side of Sloane Square. 'Do you think you can get us to Smithfield?'

'Oh yes, of course. I forgot it was so close to the market.'

'Humph.' Mimi was unconvinced.

'It's such a joy to have you around, little sister. I can give my conscience a holiday while you worry about it for me.'

'Got a job yet?'

'No,' he said defensively.

'Living off Father and Annabel still, then. No wonder you're going to marry her. I'll tell her you're only doing it for the money.'

'God, you can be a bitch, Mimi.'

Antonio stared sullenly at the road ahead and turned
the CD player up loud. George Michael drowned any conversation Mimi might have wanted to start, and they drove
on in silence.

'No, Mrs French.'

'*Oonagh!*'

'Oonagh, I'm sorry. It's this line you should be looking
at.'

'What do the brackets mean?'

'It means the company's in debt.'

'Where are the profits?'

'There aren't any because we haven't sold anything yet.'

'Why not?'

'Because tomorrow is Annabel's first show.'

'So what have you been doing since last August?'

'Preparing this show.'

'That's all? You mean I gave you all that money and all
you can show me is brackets?'

'Yes, but . . .'

'No buts, Mr Shafe. Buts make my skin crawl.'

'Mrs French, I mean Oonagh. If you look at the following page you'll see that the anticipated sales will cover
the turnover we projected in the original business plan.
Admittedly we have gone a little over budget, but Annabel
and I are perfectly aware where we have gone wrong.
Obviously when this kind of company goes through a
start-up period there are unforeseen expenditures and
extraordinary costs.'

'What are you trying to tell me, Duncan? Are you pussyfooting around the fact that you've gone massively over budget and you're saying sorry, Mummy, like a naughty little boy and you think everything'll be all right?' Oonagh reached for her handbag. 'All right. How much is it going to cost to make everything all right?'

'Nothing, Oonagh.'

'Rubbish – you just said the brackets were a serious problem.'

'No. As long as we reach target sales then we should cover ourselves for the next season.'

'And how long's a season? You and I both know a season's as long as a sneeze in fashion. It hardly gives you time.' Duncan tried not to look too exasperated.

'I hope . . .' He scratched his head, looking for words simple enough to put Oonagh off the scent. 'I hope that the next month will prove that we have a viable commercial product, and that within five years your initial investment will be repaid in full with the interest. Then you will no longer have to worry about us.'

'Worry! Darling, it's my daughter we're talking about. Are you implying that just because sooner or later she may not owe me money I'll stop worrying about her? Sweetheart,' her voice was acid, 'one's relationships with one's children are not entirely mercantile.' She stood and angrily pulled open the door. 'You accountants can think of nothing but money, that's what makes you so terminally dull. I'm tempted to pay more just to get a translator to mediate between us. I'll keep my filthy money if you

insist. But don't come running to me when it all goes hor-
ribly wrong.'

'Don't worry,' Duncan said, then added under his
breath, 'We'll avoid that at all costs.'

'What?' Oonagh's Lady Bracknell tones reverberated
round the atelier.

'I can't thank you enough for your help.' Duncan spread
as much charm as he could muster across his face and
tried to hide his relief as the front door opened to Mimi
and Antonio, the perfect antidote to Oonagh. The atmosphere in the atelier relaxed. Annabel had her best friend
and her lover to take her attention away from the fact that
the hand finishers were having trouble distressing the silk
roses they'd whipped up that morning, and that there was
only a limited amount of the lining fabric for the dresses
and the stock assistant couldn't remember where they'd
got it from. They'd never be able to make more.

'Hey.' Antonio grinned at the assembled throng. His
generosity at actually turning up was almost overwhelm-
ing him. Duncan turned his back and went to hide in his
office. He hated Antonio. Mimi tried not to look too disapproving and kissed Annabel.

'Hello, darling.' She took in Annabel's gaunt face, rest-
less eyes and hands and decided that the faster she got
Oonagh and Antonio out of the atelier and left Annabel to
get on with her job the better.

Annabel hugged her. 'You're early. I thought you
wouldn't get here till late tonight.'

'Aha – a lifetime of airline abuse sped up the journey

considerably. I was upgraded to Concorde. So, we just dropped in to say hi. We're not staying – you must have so much to do. Come on, Antonio, let's take Oonagh to lunch. We've got so much to catch up on.' Mimi took Oonagh's arm and tried to steer her towards the door.

'No, Mimi. You stay. I'll take Oonagh out. I know how much you long to stay and help, and Oonagh and I are just spare parts round here. Aren't we, Oonagh?' Antonio took Oonagh's other arm and started a little tug of war with Mimi. Oonagh didn't like playing rope.

'I'm not sure we've finished. Annabel hasn't even showed me the collection yet. I've spent all morning closeted with that terrible accountant and now I want to have some fun with my daughter. Come on, Annabel, take me through it. I'm sure you must need my advice on some finishing touches.'

Annabel looked as if she was about to burst into tears again. She took a deep breath. 'Mother, you'll find it all so boring and it's not perfect enough for you yet. Why don't you go and have lunch and come back for the rehearsal at six?'

'Well.' Oonagh sniffed, offended. 'I can tell when I'm not wanted. Come on, Antonio. You can buy me lunch. Annabel obviously needs her own mother as much as she needs an injection of arsenic! Take me to the most fashionable new place in London.' Antonio blanched. 'Don't worry, darling – it's on me. Now, where shall we go?' She marched towards the door holding Antonio in a vice-like grip. Mimi was left behind.

'Thank God she's gone.' Annabel hugged Mimi. 'Come on, I want to show you everything. I think I've solved the boring bit – but I need you to reassure me.'

'Can I try some of it on?' Mimi laughed as Annabel's face fell. 'It's all right. I'm only joking. I know I'm hardly a sample size.' She grinned across at George. 'Georgie there'll just have to run something up for me, won't you, George?' She raised an eyebrow at his worried face. 'Calm down. I'll wait till after the show if you like.'

'Ooh, such generosity in one so young.' George danced back to the roses he was drying over a fan after they'd spent the morning in a bucket of cold tea. The ageing process for the fabric was time-consuming but hardly complicated. 'You don't want to wait too long, though. I'll be in a debtors' prison at the rate I'm going.'

'Oh shut up, George. Mimi doesn't want to hear about your financial difficulties.' Annabel took Mimi by the hand and led her to the first of the outfits she'd designed for the show. 'Now, let me explain . . .'

Rehearsal. Duncan watched as thirty-five models stood, confused and cold, and waited for Annabel to give them instructions. They weren't getting any of those because Antonio was throwing a little petulant tantrum front of house and Annabel was trying to calm him down instead of concentrating on the fact that at nine thirty the next morning a few of the fashion cognoscenti might actually deign to turn up at such a down-market and unimportant event; the first show of a new, unknown designer.

'Why can't I sit here?'

'Because that's where the important journalists sit.'

'But they aren't here.'

'I'm not talking about now. I'm talking about tomorrow morning.'

'Well, there's no guarantee they'll turn up then. Surely you'd do better to give the seat to a committed participant than keep them for a bunch of battered old hags who've got nothing better to do on a Thursday morning.'

'Antonio, please. Why do you have to be spoilt about it?'

'I'm not being spoilt, I'm being honest. It's much better to be prepared for disappointment – that way you can only be pleased with the way things go, and not miserable. I'm just warning you not to get your hopes up too high. I'm only doing it for your own good.'

'Thanks for the support.'

'I *am* being supportive. I'm here, aren't I?'

'Well, don't be if you can't be a bit more positive for me. You're behaving as if you're jealous.'

'Why should I be jealous? Really, Annabel, I'd have thought it perfectly obvious that your career leaves me absolutely cold. I love you for your beauty, not for your arguable talents as a dressmaker, and I'm just trying to make you see that you should love yourself for the same reasons. I mean, until tomorrow you don't even know if you're any good, therefore you should be prepared for disappointment.' He shrugged dolefully. 'I think I'm being rather constructive, actually.'

Annabel quashed the temptation to thump him and marched off to the models to start the rehearsal. 'Bastard' might or might not have been the word that slipped from her lips. Antonio couldn't be sure.

The venue for this great event was Marylebone Station, the one railway terminal that hadn't been ruined by what had once been British Rail. Duncan often wondered whether they'd kept what an efficient estate agent would have called an 'original feature' as an emergency earner for the railway system. If all else failed they could rent out the station for anything other than trains and passengers and perhaps some money might make it into the coffers of the fast collapsing British railway system. At the rate the station was charging Annabel for her show, Duncan was surprised they allowed trains to stop at the platforms at all. They could have made a fortune hosting other, more marketable events rather than getting the British public to and from London.

Front of house was less front than side. The audience were to sit along the edge of the platform as the girls wound their way between them towards one enticingly open door of a resurrected locomotive, which had been rented at a cost of twice the company's salary budget for that year. Duncan wasn't going to complain. How could he have turned Annabel down when she'd explained carefully that the enormous expense would be returned a thousandfold during the post-show sales period?

'Annabel, darling. I'm sorry to hurry you, but I've got a dinner.' Pandora Williams, the only supermodel to be doing the show, tossed her raven hair away from her face and dragged pointedly on her Marlboro.

Annabel jumped. 'I'm sorry about the delay, everyone. OK, let's get started.' She turned her back on Antonio, and he slumped into his space next to an equally grumpy Oonagh and pointedly opened a book.

Late that night George sat nervously eating beans on toast and staring at the three rather worn outfits that he might be able to get away with the next day when the phone rang.

'George?'

'Annabel — what's the matter?'

'I'm just warning you, darling — if you bring up the fact that you don't think I pay you enough one more time then you'll find yourself with a pay cut before I throw you out on your ear.'

'But Annabel . . .'

'No buts, George. How dare you embarrass me like that in front of Mimi?'

'I was joking.'

'Well, it wasn't funny. I'll see you at the atelier first thing. And you'd better not let me down tomorrow or you might find your trial period being renewed again.' The line went dead.

George sat down heavily, shaking. He loved his job, but Annabel could be quite a tough taskmistress.

Chapter 3

THE Show. Annabel stood backstage, exquisite in a steel-grey suit, a huge pale pink silk rose pinned to the tightly nipped in waist, her lips blue with cold and nerves, and tried to stop staring at the empty VIP first-row seats that lined her rented platform at Marylebone Station. Her friends had turned up, her mother and Antonio and Gladstone were making a fantastic row along their section of the front row, but there were no VIPs. The fact that the only supermodel who'd agreed to do her show hadn't turned up yet didn't bother her. With no VIPs, what was the point of doing the show at all?

'Boo!'

Annabel leapt out of her skin. 'Pandora!' Her super-model had arrived. 'Where the fuck have you been?'

'Darling, I'm sorry, but the alarm clock didn't go off.'

Pandora drew her coat closer around herself. 'Now, where's my rack? I hope you'll let me keep my thermals on. It's bloody freezing in here.'

'I don't care what you do as long as you sell my clothes for me. Go on – you're over there.'

Pandora kissed the top of Annabel's head. 'Don't worry, darling – I'll be fabulous.' She skipped off to find the party dresses she was due to model.

Front of house Oonagh held court.

'I'm not sure I would have done *exactly* the same thing.' Her voice rang across the rafters of the station. 'But the young today . . .'

'Mother, shut up.' Kenneth sat staring sullenly ahead. 'You're so embarrassing.'

'Darling, the only way I'm going to keep warm is by talking. Honestly, floor-length mink usually does the trick, but today it feels as if I've turned up in a bikini to sit here. Gladstone,' she clasped his knee, 'what do you think?' There was no answer. He was deep in whispered conversation with Jean-Luc, resplendent in a brand-new Nicole Farhi suit. 'Gladstone, please . . . What do you think?'

'I think she's stunning.' His face lit up as a radiant and heavily pregnant redhead strode into the arena, part of the retinue of Nina Charles, editor in chief of the biggest UK fashion magazine and general star of the fashion firmament who'd turned up with her entire team. Annabel's staff breathed a sigh of relief. If no other VIPs came, at least the most powerful fashion editor in the UK was

there. As long as she liked the show then the end of the
world could not be as near as they'd feared.

The first, haunting notes of Elgar's cello concerto
floated out, and finally the show began.

Luckily the music was loud enough to drown Oonagh's
running commentary. 'Oh dear, what is this? Does she
think it's a re-run of the last night of the Proms?' was her
opening line. Duncan could have killed her.

'Help, help, help, la-la-la-la, dum, dum.' Duncan sang
tunelessly as he put the finishing touches to the antique
shop in Mount Street which had been borrowed for the
post-show sales period and transformed into a showroom.
He'd waited until the show had started and the first of the
felt suits had made it down the runway before leaving. He
hadn't been able to bear standing there until the end in
case it was a disaster. He didn't really know what he was
doing playing with arrangements of camellias, either. His
role was accounting, not interior decorating, but if there
was one thing he hated about his job it was that it kept him
away from the real action of the business. He wasn't
expected to be interested, and his opinion was irrelevant.
He straightened his tie in front of the mirror. For the first
time in his life he wished he looked less like a prop forward at Sedbergh school and more like a fop – Kenneth,
for instance. No, it'd be physically impossible for him to
be made to look so emasculated and in his wildest dreams
he'd never wear pink velvet.

He was washing up his coffee mug in the back room

when he heard the first people back from the show barge into the shop. Kenneth and Jean-Luc were arguing as usual.

'I hate her,' whined Kenneth.

Jean-Luc posed carefully on a Chippendale sofa covered in dark African violet damask rented for the occasion, choosing it over an armchair because the purple was better with the buttercup linen silk mix of his new suit. 'You don't really,' he told Kenneth. 'She's your muzzer. You are a muzzer's boy srew and srew. Don't try and make me believe that you can't stand the sight of 'er enough to do anysing about it.'

Kenneth attempted a careful sitting down in the manner of Jean-Luc and failed entirely. The tails of his black velvet Yohji Nehru jacket would be desperately creased when he stood up. Jean-Luc looked at his lover with distaste. Kenneth was too busy checking his shoes for marks and polishing any tiny blemishes he found with a lace-trimmed handkerchief to notice.

'What can I do? She follows me around day and night banging on about her stupid little boyfriend, spending all her money on him and what little's left on Annabel. All I get out of it is the occasional loan of a credit card. I mean, why should I love her? She left us with Nanny Palls until she died and we had both left school, and then the only time she saw us was when she sent for us to act as accessories to her stupid little life. Who wouldn't hate a mother who did that?'

'Well, if you 'ate 'er zat much why don't you do

somesing about it?' Jean-Luc's accent was so ridiculous Duncan wondered if it was put on specially.

'Just watch me. I will. You'll see. You'll love me even more then, won't you? Imagine, all that money and never having to ask for it.' Kenneth sulkily pared his fingernails with a small bejewelled dagger which he'd swiped off a handy shelf.

'I sink you're wonderful already, darling. I love you so much I could eat you for breakfast. And I love you even more if you do ziss sing for me, just to prove 'ow brave you are. I sink it is a wonderfool idea. But 'ow are you going to do it?'

'Wait and see, my precious. Wait and see. My plan is almost perfect and when I've got it down pat I'll tell you all about it. I know how excited you get when I talk about it. I want to draw it out for as long as possible.'

'Darlings – wasn't it wonderful?' Oonagh burst into the room brandishing a bottle of Bollinger in a threatening manner.

Duncan crept out of his hiding place and made as if to sneak out. Kenneth stared at him, horrified. Duncan must have heard every word he and Jean-Luc had said. His blood ran cold through his veins. Fear gripped him until he looked at Jean-Luc, who was staring at Oonagh greedily, licking his lips. Kenneth relaxed. If Jean-Luc wasn't frightened then neither was he.

'Glasses, money man,' Oonagh ordered.

Duncan instinctively checked his bifocals.

Oonagh sighed dramatically. 'Ooh, darling, no wonder

you're an accountant. Not very gifted in the lateral thinking department, are you?' She waved the champagne in his
face. '*Champagne* glasses . . . please?' She giggled coquet-
tishly, threw her floor-length mink onto the nearest chair
and eased herself onto the sofa between her son and
his boyfriend. 'So, boys, what were you discussing so
earnestly before I so rudely interrupted you?' Without
waiting for an answer, she launched into a review of
Annabel's show.

'Didn't like the pink party dresses much – did you? A
touch on the passé side, I thought. Not so much last
season as last decade. Still, I suppose she's learning. Now,
if she'd given them sleeves then they might have been a
tiny touch more wearable, but nobody reveals their arms
these days, do they. At least nobody with enough money
to buy those things. You know, I overheard the buyer
from Harvey Nicks talking about retail prices of over
£4,000, and all for a scrap of lining material. And don't
tell me you're paying for the creative impulse behind. I
happen to know that that lovely little George ran those up
himself only yesterday afternoon, and they were hemmed
this morning. I really don't know what I'll order for
myself. I suppose the dove-grey dévoré Pandora wore
would do for something. No wonder Annabel refused to
show me the collection in advance. There's nothing there
for me – and as I'm her target market I don't think she's
been very bright.'

She paused for breath and Duncan returned with a tray
of filled champagne glasses. Oonagh took one from him

without acknowledging him. 'I suppose she's still young — she needs time to mature. If she's not careful that silly little accountant will keep on presenting me with brackets and the money will just dry up. I'm not made of the stuff, you know.' Her tinkling laughter threatened to bring down the chandelier above her.

'Annabel — darling! It was too wonderful!' Oonagh gushed, as her daughter appeared at the door, flanked by Nina Charles and Rory Williams, fashion gurus extraordinaire.

Duncan kept his head down and made his way to the door, wondering how Oonagh managed to be so sycophantic about something that plainly made her jealous as hell. It was time for him to get back to the office and take advantage of the peace and quiet to do some of his own work. He was happy to go, leaving Annabel to enjoy her success. She had walked into the showroom laughing, pure joy for her own achievement shining from her eyes. He would leave her until she needed him next. And as for Kenneth and Jean-Luc, they were plainly mad — weren't they?

Duncan wasn't the only person to sneak out of the showroom. Jean-Luc and Kenneth escaped as soon as they could, which was pretty quickly on account of the fact that they were totally superfluous to requirements. Their destination? Why, a little Lebanese restaurant in Shepherd Market, of course. And who were they there to meet? Not Gladstone and Antonio! Really, what have this little quartet of champagne and unsavouries got up their designer sleeves? Well, Gladstone had been seconded by Oonagh to keep a weather eye on Kenneth, and he and Antonio were taking the opportunity to wheedle whatever it was that Kenneth and Jean-Luc were planning out of them. They'd decided that Lebanese food, a particular favourite with Jean-Luc, and lunchtime champagne, a particular favourite of Kenneth's, would provide the perfect ingredients for forcing a confession.

'I don't see why Mummy has to be so bitchy about Annabel's collection. I thought it was lovely.' Kenneth was being unusually loyal to his older sister.

'Dreamy, darling. If I had a better waist I'd order one of zose lovely pink party dresses myself. There's nossing wrong with my arms zat a little occasional waxing doesn't solve and I am her target market, aren't I, with you as my paymaster?' Jean-Luc batted his eyelashes at his lunch companions.

Antonio simply snapped back, 'Do you never leave your camp persona behind?' While he picked grumpily at a Lebanese delicacy in a bowl in the middle of the table.

Gladstone shot him a look reminding him to shut up and concentrate on the business in hand, and turned to placate the bristling Jean-Luc. 'Ignore him, darling. Just remember his interests are exactly in tune with ours.'

'Precisely.' Kenneth, who had no real idea of what was going on, pouted at Antonio. 'He's just a greasy little South American who needs us much more than we need him.'

Antonio bared his teeth and growled behind the protective screen of his menu. Why had he agreed to the Lebanese food idea anyway? He hated the stuff. He lowered the menu. 'Look, guys, let's cut the crap and get down to business, shall we?'

'Only if you stop using gangster language. This isn't Chicago in the thirties, you know.' Kenneth smiled sweetly at his potential brother-in-law. 'Besides, what *is* the business? I thought we were just having lunch together to escape from all those awful fashion groupies. Ugh, did you see the way that George sidled up to Rory Williams and patted him on the backside? As if they even knew each other. I mean, George is just an assistant, and Rory's Nina's archangel Gabriel at that lovely magazine of hers. They're hardly in the same league, are they? Who does George think he is?'

'I thought with you lot it didn't matter whether you'd been formally introduced or not.' Antonio was curious.

'Darling, not all of us slum it with just anybody, you know,' Kenneth snapped.

'No,' Antonio replied, smiling through sharp white teeth at Jean-Luc. 'Just some of you.'

'Oh stop bitching, darling. Anyone would sink you were jealous of us. I sink you should calm yourself before someone gets the wrong idea. Or is it ze right idea?' Jean-Luc looked at Antonio and Gladstone.

Antonio looked as if he was about to explode. Kenneth poured a second glass of champagne and settled down to some serious drinking.

'So, boys, what's going on?' Antonio said, when he'd got his temper under control.

'Jump in feet first, why don't you?' bristled Gladstone.

'Listen, I'm curious and I thought I'd ask. How were you going to bring it up, Gladstone? These people hardly react well to subtlety – you know how things have to be spelt out in words of one syllable for Kenneth.'

'Not that bluntly.'

'What are you talking about?' Kenneth asked. 'I'm not stupid! I know you're talking about me.'

'Well done, Sherlock. Well, you clever little thing, we just want to know what's going on. What are you two planning? We're dying to know. Whatever it is, perhaps we can help.'

'I don't sink so.' Jean-Luc jabbed at some couscous with a sliver of pitta bread in a manner intended to suggest that they change the subject.

'Come on, you can tell us. What is it? Are you going to steal all Oonagh's money?'

'Or take over Annabel's company?'

'Or get a job each?'

'Or move to the other side of the world so we can all be rid of you?'

'Face it, boys. Something's going on and we're going to get it out of you one way or another. You've been giggling and whispering to each other like school children planning a classroom coup for weeks.'

'I know!' Antonio's face lit up. 'You're going to kill Oonagh.' He burst out laughing.

Kenneth blanched; Jean-Luc blushed. Gladstone and Antonio stared at their lunch companions.

'You *are* going to kill Oonagh.' Antonio was amazed. 'You're not really?'

'Why?' Gladstone couldn't help asking.

'Because she's spent a lifetime putting me down and telling me I'm stupid, and because I hate her and Jean-Luc hates her, and she's a waste of space and won't give me any money, which isn't fair because it's mine really and not hers. It was my father's money and should have come directly to me. She shouldn't have anything to do with it – let alone be able to tell me where or when I can spend any of it. I'm fed up with her and I'm going to kill her as a punishment.' Kenneth sounded like the petulant child he was.

'A punishment.' Gladstone was fascinated. 'A punishment for what?'

'For not letting us anywhere near her until we were grown up and for leaving us with Nanny Palls and for now treating me with less respect than she gives Madame de Pompadour.'

Kenneth thumped the table and fought back tears for his own tragic state. 'I'll teach all of you to think I'm stupid. Killing people isn't easy, you know. It requires planning, strategy and skill – all of which I'm going to prove I have. And when I've got all the money then you'll all have to be nice to me for a change instead of ignoring me and sucking up to her all the time.' He looked pointedly at Gladstone.

'Who's Madame de Pompadour?' Antonio was understandably confused.

'Her Pekinese,' Gladstone said, his eyebrows raised to suggest that Kenneth was naturally mad having inherited lunacy from a woman who'd call a Chinese dog after a French royal mistress.

'So you're really planning on doing away with her — how?' Antonio asked, nonchalantly picking bits from between his teeth. Neither he nor Gladstone believed for one second that Kenneth would ever commit an act as violent as murder, let alone get together a plan for it.

'That's none of your business. But you wait and see. She's not long for this world.'

'Oh, don't be ridiculous. You've got the gumption of a wet rag. You'd never do anything so stupid.'

'Don't call *me* stupid, Gladstone,' Kenneth retorted. 'You're the stupid one. You backed the wrong horse. I should start painting if I were you. You'll be out of a job sooner than you think.'

'I'll be OK,' Gladstone sneered.

'Yeah? Your studio at home's full of nothing but your stereo and that stupid guitar you pretend you can play. You'll soon find out what it's like to be a starving artist in a garret, just you wait and see.'

'My God — you're serious,' Antonio whispered.

'At last you're listening, Antonio.'

'I can't *believe* you told zem.' Jean-Luc whined furiously.

But the Yohji-clad Little Lord Fauntleroy lookalike just smiled at his lover.

'Don't worry, darling, if anyone round here lacks gumption it's those two. They won't tell anyone because they don't think I'm up to it. They'll just watch from the sidelines, looking forward to my failure. Well, you shouldn't be so sure of yourselves, boys, because I'm going to show you. I'm a man with a purpose which I intend to achieve.'

Kenneth went on to list ways by which his mother might meet an untimely death. Admittedly she was unlikely to be pushed off a mountain as the logistics of getting her up it would be too daunting, but poison and strangling were possibilities. Jean-Luc suggested poisoning with lipstick and strangling with ropes of Chanel pearls.

'How does it feel to be a star?'

'Darling, it was a key moment in time, it was a new beginning for the industry as a whole. Watch out – this girl is going everywhere!'

'No, I think the Schiaparelli influence is overrated. There is a little Balenciaga there, but if you ask me she's gone straight back to early twentieth-century photographs and moved on from there. I mean, if you think of the emancipation of women over the century and put that all into the perspective of thirty models in a show, where does it leave you?'

Non sequiturs buzzed about the showroom as George unpacked the collection and tried to make sure that nobody stole anything. After all, fashion people were notoriously badly paid and a loose jacket could easily end up in somebody's bag.

Annabel sat in state in an armchair in the centre of the room, receiving the people who came and bowed over her hand and took three-minute soundbites for their shows, their papers, their magazines. Gay Smith, an unattractive paparazzo whose success lay largely in the fact that she was short enough to elbow her way through any crowd, darted about photographing not only Annabel but all the fashion royalty who came to pay court. Annabel shone with success and relief. Duncan was right. Her success would be her protection, just for the day.

Saul Smytheson, the fashionable photographer of the moment, arrived with his new lover, an Italian interior decorator called Gianfranco Desire.

'Darling – fabulous!'

'Spectacular. Shall we?'

'Oh, I think so.'

'We're having a little party.'

'Milan – next week.'

'Will you come?'

'It won't be anything without you.'

'Just you, I think.' George had been hovering hopefully. 'Just you – and perhaps Mimi?'

'Mimi?'

'Only if she promises to giggle all evening in that charming way of hers.'

'I'll think about it.'

'Do, darling. *Ciao*.'

Rory Williams and Nina Charles had stayed for over an

hour, showing a solidarity and goodwill not usually extended to a new designer. Rory was after the free champagne, of course, and he and Gianfranco were old friends. But Nina's presence showed that Annabel had arrived and would be on the scene for more than the average five minutes. For Nina gave sound bites too and backed the new designer all the way.

Even Gloria Wharton gave in to peer pressure and arrived looking annoyed.

And Annabel, being as gifted a saleswoman as she was a designer, charmed her.

'George, can you hold all calls and tell anyone who comes that I'm busy for an hour? Gloria Wharton's here.' Gloria preened – recognition for her talents was much appreciated. 'Gloria, may I show you the collection? I know you had another meeting and couldn't make the show. I'd love to tell you the story of it.' Annabel was positively unctuous and Gloria lapped it up.

'She could always offer to lick her boots,' George muttered.

'No, I think not. Mimi covered it, didn't she?' Gloria was ruthlessly dismissive.

'Yes, she was there.'

'Well, she can shoot it for us then, can't she? I'm sure she can fill me in. I don't think I actually have to see anything. I just dropped by to . . .'

Yes! This was definitely a game in two halves and between them Annabel and Mimi had won. Annabel itched to go and call Mimi on her mobile. Restraining herself, she poured a glass of champagne and held fire for later.

'My first collection's going to hit the American news-stands before the stores get it. Don't you understand, Mimi? Now Bergdorfs and Barneys and Neimans and Saks'll have to buy it and I'll be a millionaire before Christmas.' Annabel paused for breath. 'And then she said you could shoot it!'

'I'm amazed. In fact I think you're lying. She hasn't called me.'

'Don't be ridiculous. She knows you're my best friend so she'd never have told me you could shoot the collection unless she meant it. Maybe she hasn't got your mobile number?'

'Yeah, right. If she really wanted me to shoot it I'd know about it by now somehow.'

'Not necessarily. I mean, you rushed from show to show all afternoon, never less than four rows behind her – four rows is a long way in fashion.'

'Thanks for reminding me quite how lowly a position I hold, Annabel. And as for the shoot, I wouldn't count any chickens.'

'Me count chickens? My, your imagination's more pro-lific than mine. But passing on messages is my other vocation. You know I always wanted to be a receptionist.'

'Calm down quickly before I see you rushing off to the nearest employment agency.'

Annabel and Mimi were revelling in a post mortem of

the day over a large jug of Moscow Mules at the Smithfield atelier. Their first glasses of the stuff were only half empty. They hadn't seen each other for four months – they had a lot of catching up to do.

'So how's New York, Mimi? Do you like working for Gloria? Do you think Barneys'll give me some windows? Will you ask the market editor to get onto them?'

'I hate working for Gloria. She and Don Elson leave the offices running with slime every day. And Barneys might give you windows if we have enough pages in the magazine.'

'I wish you'd taken the job Nina offered you in London. But then you wouldn't be shooting my lovely clothes for the American market, would you?'

'I love living in New York. Admit – it's worth working for those two creeps if I get an apartment in Manhattan to match me and not them.'

'I'll let you know when I run out of enthusiasm for Europe. Have you worked with Saul yet? Maybe he'll take the pictures of my collection. I know they only look like happy snaps but I'll be so famous as a result . . .'

'Haven't had the honour. You know he's given up the All American Cowboy look and gone for a sort of Far East meets Australian surfer thing – it's really frightening. Nobody's sure if the little cap's supposed to be Chinese or something for swimming in.'

'I know. He came to the showroom this afternoon with a large weirdo in a real fur coat.'

'That'd be Gianfranco Desire.'

'They asked me to a party in Milan next week.'

'Good – we can go together.'

Mimi took a slug from her Moscow Mule. 'Right.' She reached into her capacious Gucci holdall and pulled out a large yellow legal pad. 'Since we're here and on our own we may as well get this over with now.'

'Get what over with?' Annabel was so tired and excited at the same time that she could hardly focus on Mimi, let alone take in the fact that her friend had started writing a list on her pad. She took a slug of her drink and poured most of it down her shirt. 'Shit!'

'The interview.'

'What interview?'

'Oh, darling – you've just done the show of the century. You are the flavour of the season. If you weren't holed up here with the phones turned off you'd be being swamped already – look at the rate of paper pouring through the fax machine!' Mimi pointed through the open door of the administration office at the pile of paper falling to the floor. 'If I don't interview you now I'm never going to get near you again. You know what fame in this business is like. I'd better make the most of you now in case it's all over next season.'

'Thanks a bunch. But you know everything there is to know about me already. Besides, I've been interviewed nonstop all day. I love talking about the collection but there's nothing about it or me that you don't already know.' Annabel dabbed at her shirt with little success. Sticky lime drink was there to stay.

'If you honestly think Gloria wants me to shoot you and your pretty little dresses then I'd better ask all those pertinent questions now.'

'I keep telling you, Mimi – you know all the answers already. Besides, you should be careful – you don't want to be seen trying too hard. I mean, Gloria might make you part of her inner circle.'

'Yuck – can you imagine? She's so dreadful. She bought her position by sleeping with the group editorial director, who we all know is the slimeball of the century. She's useless at her job. She used to be great when she worked for Nina because Nina kept her in check and made sure her ideas were vaguely feasible. Now she's editor in chief of the American magazine it's as if she's got editor's block – her ideas have dried up and she can't seem to manage her staff. She knows perfectly well just how precarious her situation is, otherwise she wouldn't mind people creeping up behind her. I mean, you should have seen her face when I sat down beside her on the flight over. I thought she was going to have heart seizure.' Mimi looked up as she took another slug of her drink. Annabel had collapsed over the table and was fast asleep. 'I must be so fascinating,' she said to her recumbent friend, and began to make up Annabel's answers to her questions.

By now Kenneth was falling-down drunk, whether from fear of actually carrying out a lifetime of threats to kill his mother or from pure joy nobody really cared. Jean-Luc steered him down the stairs from the little flat above the restaurant where the four men had met at lunchtime and leaned him against the wall while he opened the door. Once the door was open Kenneth slid inexorably down and landed in a mess spotlit by the street light. Duncan, of course, was across the road in his flat, not quite curtain twitching but, as he often did, staring blindly into the street. His dream was of a world which included neither Oonagh nor fashion shows but just him and Annabel running a successful business, having lots of children and living in a house with a garden full of beech trees.

'Aahh!' screeched Kenneth. 'I'm going to murder her in the morning,' he slurred.

'Kenneth, get up, please . . .' Jean-Luc flapped his arms around hopelessly. There was no way he was about to get down in the gutter to rescue his lover, however much it might be financially worth his while. He was wearing brand-new buttercup Nicole Farhi after all.

In his little flat across the road Duncan, coming round from his dream of Annabel in his own personal utopia, blinked at the sight of Kenneth's white-blond hair reflecting light from the street lamp. It took him a couple of seconds before he realised who he was looking at.

'Oh shit.' He shrugged on an old green corduroy jacket and headed out to help, forgetting his keys as he went and tripping on the last stair of his building so that as he came to the rescue Jean-Luc shrank back in horror thinking they were being attacked by a madman. Before he had time to run off and abandon Kenneth, Duncan managed to pant, 'What's going on? What's wrong with him?'

'Oh darling,' gushed Jean-Luc. 'Sank God you are 'ere. What am I to do wizz ziss person?'

'Get him in a taxi and take him home, I should think,' Duncan grunted as he tried to pull Kenneth upright.

'Ooh, we are witty ziss evening.' Jean-Luc gave Duncan a manic grin. 'And where do you suggest finding a taxi here at ziss time of ze night?'

Duncan propped Kenneth up against the street lamp. 'I suppose I could help you get him to Piccadilly. It's only round the corner.' So much for Duncan's quiet night. Not only was he going to have to drag this twerp around the streets of London in the middle of the night but he'd locked himself out of his flat and he was going to have to go to the atelier to get his spare keys. He hoped somebody would be there. Duncan dragged one of Kenneth's arms around his shoulders and headed down towards Piccadilly. Jean-Luc obviously had no intention of helping. Giggling and prancing around in his yellow silk, he looked like a drugged circus monkey.

'Ha, ha. What luck zat you arrived just at ze moment opportune.'

'I live across the road. I happened to see you.' Duncan could hardly speak under Kenneth's dead weight.

'No – 'ow surprising! I would have sought you'd live somewhere more . . .' There was a long pause before Jean-Luc whispered the word 'suburban' as if he were uttering something of the utmost profanity.

'Really.' Duncan couldn't care less what this mincing little fool thought of him.

'Yes, really.' Jean-Luc raised a quizzical eyebrow which Duncan found so contrived he would quite happily have split it with a right hook had he not been bowed under the weight of the drunken Kenneth. 'Do you spend a lot of time staring out of the window ready to rescue damsels in distress?' Jean-Luc enquired.

'Yeah, every evening. Been a bit short on the damsel front recently so I thought I'd practise on you two. What were you doing in that tart's flat anyway?'

'Why, celebrating Annabel's achievement, of course.'

'How stimulating for you both.'

The lights were still on at the atelier. Duncan breathed a sigh of relief, told the taxi driver to wait and rang the street bell praying that someone would answer the door.

'Yes?' Mimi's voice was nervous. Who would be trying to get into the atelier at this hour?

'Mimi? It's Duncan. I'm locked out. Can you let me in?'

'If I can find the buzzer thing.' The door clicked open and Duncan ran up the stairs two at a time.

'Thank God you're here.' He rushed past a confused Mimi and grabbed a tenner out of the petty cash tin in his desk drawer. 'Don't lock the door behind me,' he called as he headed back downstairs. 'I'm coming back.'

Mimi sat back down at the atelier table and began to collect her papers together. She'd put Annabel to bed on the sofa in the reception area and covered her in both their coats. Annabel had slept the sleep of the truly exhausted while Mimi wrote up the report of Annabel's show and made up the interview. Now Mimi thanked God for Duncan's opportune arrival. It meant that she wouldn't have to wake Annabel; she could let her sleep as long as she liked. After all, a midnight crisis was ideal timing for her to get to know Duncan better. She tucked her exuberant curls behind her ears, smoothed the tiny gold sweater she'd grabbed on an emergency shopping spree at Joseph the previous afternoon and hoped that the black trousers she'd bought there weren't so tight he'd be put off for ever. Pinching her cheeks to add colour to her face she waited, trying to look cool, for his return.

'Thanks,' Duncan panted as he slumped in the chair Annabel had occupied earlier. He looked at the dregs of her Moscow Mule with distaste, drank them and poured himself more from the leftovers in the jug.

'I can make more if you like?'

'What?'

'Moscow Mules. I've got the kit in my bag. I don't think there's any more ice, but warm, fresh and fizzy might be better than warm and flat as a pancake.'

'Thanks. Don't worry. I don't know why I'm drinking this really. I should just go home now I've got my keys.'

'What happened?'

'I locked myself out.'

'How irritating.'

'Bloody nightmare. And it's all the fault of her stupid little brother.' He pointed at the recumbent form of Annabel on the sofa.

'Why? What's he done now?'

'He fell out of a house of ill repute across the road from my flat and I saw him. Jean-Luc looked as if he was about to walk off and leave him so I thought I'd better help. Where this Good Samaritan instinct comes from I have no idea. Frankly I think they both deserve to rot in the gutter. Still, Annabel would have been furious if I'd just left them to it. So I went to help and forgot my keys and the door slammed behind me. I came over here in the vague hope that someone would be around to let me in. I keep my spare keys here, you see. But that's no good really because my house keys and my office keys are on the same ring, so if I'm locked out of my flat I'm locked out of the office too.' He looked up and smiled. 'I'm sorry. I'm rambling. It's something that happens when I'm suffering from absolute exhaustion.'

'What?' Mimi blushed. She hadn't listened to a word he'd said. She'd been daydreaming about running her hands through his wiry hair and pushing off his jacket and shirt to see how sturdy his frame really was under his clothes. 'Sorry. I wasn't concentrating.'

'Don't worry. It was mostly rubbish anyway.' Duncan turned and looked at Annabel. 'Is she all right?'

'Exhausted. She passed out while I was talking to her earlier. I hadn't the heart to wake her and take her home so I've been doing a bit of work. Everyone else seems shattered, but I've got jet lag so I think it's about time to go out for the evening and I'm not a bit tired.' She looked at Duncan brightly and just caught herself in time before she batted her eyelashes and did a questioning, suggestive tilt of her head.

'Did she enjoy today? I mean, did it go well? I know so little about fashion shows – it's hard to tell really, isn't it?'

'What?'

'If something's the success of the season or a flop.'

'Oh, I wouldn't worry about it. I think success of the season is probably a bit premature as we haven't even got to Milan yet, but she's certainly the toast of London. We shouldn't really be here. I should be dragging her around all the parties so that she can be fêted and photographed as every true fashion success should. But she can't. Not tonight, anyway. She was close to tears all afternoon while she was being interviewed. Elsa Klench had to lend her a handkerchief at one point.'

'Who's Elsa Klench?'

'CNN.'

'Oh. I thought CNN covered wars?'

'And a little light fashion to give a balance.'

'I didn't know.'

Mimi began to fidget. The conversation had run out because she fancied Duncan rotten and she was always tongue-tied with potential lovers. On the other hand she was wide awake and dreading a sleepless night in Antonio's huge, characterless apartment. It was time to take the bull by the horns.

'Look, why don't you help me take Annabel home? She can't sleep on the sofa all night. She'll feel terrible tomorrow if she doesn't get some proper sleep in her own

bed and get up to her own bathroom. Then we could go
for a drink somewhere? Or get something to eat. I don't
suppose you're hungry, are you?'

Duncan laughed. 'Funnily enough I'm starving. Let's
take Annabel home and then I'll give you bacon and eggs
at my flat if you like. I don't think we'll get much else at
this time of night. London may be the happening place to
be at the moment but they don't quite have twenty-four
hour delis like you do in Manhattan.'

Mimi jumped to her feet. 'You may have a point there.
Come on, I'm starving. Oh shit.'

'What?'

'We'll never get a cab at this time of night.'

'Fuck it – let's call one and charge it to the company.'
Duncan grinned. He liked this bouncy little friend of
Annabel's, and maybe if he had dinner with her he'd pluck
up the courage to ask her whether she thought he had a
chance in hell with the sleeping blonde bombshell on the
sofa.

'Sorry about the mess.'

'Bachelor apartments are always the same.' Mimi
couldn't stop herself from picking up the books that were
strewn around Duncan's chair and making a pile of them.

He returned from the kitchen with a bottle of wine.
'Please don't clear up. Glass of wine?'

'Thanks.' Mimi sank into Duncan's armchair and curled
her legs under her, looking about her as she did so. 'This
is a lovely apartment.'

'A bit battered, I'm afraid.'

'You should get everything restored.' She eyed a chipped and ring-stained Georgian side table greedily.

'I'm saving up.'

'I'm afraid you'll have a long wait if you're going to wait for Annabel to pay for all this.'

'I don't know' – Annabel thinks we're going to be millionaires by the end of the week.'

'Hmm . . . Fashion's fickle, you know. Why do you do it? You could make enough at some accountancy firm to refurbish this place and take you on glamorous holidays and anything else you'd like.'

'I suffer from a congenital fear of being bored.'

'Really?'

'Or of being boring. I may only be an accountant but at least I work in a stimulating business. It calms my mother down.'

'Where does she come into it?'

'She can't bear my being a professional. I come from a long line of increasingly faded gentry. We live in small battered houses playing musical instruments at each other and lamenting our lost riches by disapproving of the Oonaghs of this world. I'm not supposed to know how to earn a living, let alone try too hard.'

'You'd better not let your mother see you tearing your hair out over your computer at the atelier then. She'd be horrified.'

'No chance of that – she only comes to London to buy books and see the doctor.'

'I see what you mean by old-fashioned.'

'Hmm . . . Do you like your eggs scrambled, fried or poached?'

'Poached, please. Can I do anything?' Mimi followed Duncan to the kitchen, relieved to find it clean if not exactly arranged to World of Interiors standards.

'No, no. Why don't you choose some music and put it on. I'm sorry if you don't like classical – there's nothing else, I'm afraid.'

'Then I'll just have to educate myself, shan't I?' Mimi sat on the floor and began to go through the shelves of compact discs wondering how on earth she was going to pick one when she had no idea what any of them would be like. She plumped for the Elgar cello concerto – at least after Annabel's show she knew where she'd be with that one.

'Marianita, what on earth are you doing awake at this time of night?'

'Oh *Mamà*, I couldn't sleep. I'm in Antonio's horrid apartment and it's so cold I thought I'd ring you to warm myself up.' Mimi sat on a white sofa in Antonio's sitting room, wrapped in a white duvet and holding a black telephone, staring at the bare white walls broken only by the black of the fireplace decorated with hundreds of stiff black and white invitations. It was odd that none of them was for Annabel as well. Mimi would have thought they were enough of a couple to be invited everywhere together, but evidently not.

'Where's Antonio?'

'I've no idea. He's not with Annabel – I put her to bed earlier myself.'

'Well, darling, you know what men are like. I expect he's playing bridge somewhere and is having a lucky run.'

'*Bridge?*'

'It's possible! How was the show?'

'Fantastic.'

'And how's Annabel?'

'Exhausted. Duncan and I carried her home and put her to bed earlier. She hardly even noticed us manhandling her up the stairs.'

'Duncan and I ?'

'Don't sound so worried, *Mamà*. We were both awake and so we went and had some supper, that's all.'

'Hmm, really. And where did you eat at this time of night?'

'His flat in Shepherd Market. He made me bacon and eggs and we drank a rather small glass of wine each before he called me a cab and made it quite clear he'd like to go to bed – on his own.'

'Well, I'm glad you didn't stay there and you managed to remember your background and drag yourself back to your brother's flat.'

'Don't be so old-fashioned, *Mamà*.'

'Tell me about his apartment then. What did you cook for him?'

'*Mamà*, I told you already. *He* cooked. Bacon and eggs and claret on a very battered dining room table jammed into the corner of his sitting room. The flat's beautiful. You'd be impressed. He said his uncle left it to him with all the furniture. You know, he's got some very nice pictures.'

'I can hear the cash register going in your voice, darling.'

'Yes, but he's got no cash of his own, so everything looks as if it could spend a year or two at a restorer's before it could really glow. Honestly, the kitchen's pre-war and the wallpaper's original Victorian gold and red stripes. I'm sure some museum would buy the paper off him and then he could restore the furniture with the proceeds.'

'So why doesn't he?'

'Well, he hasn't thought of that, has he?'

'And you didn't suggest it?'

'I thought that might seem a touch aggressive, *Mamà*, considering there's no real relationship there . . . yet.'

'And nor will there be if I have anything to do with it. And he obviously agrees with me, judging by the way he sent you home.'

'He was tired, *Mamà*. Besides, I would have gone home anyway. I haven't had my legs waxed for weeks.'

'You shouldn't let yourself go, Marianita.'

'Anyway, I wouldn't worry too much. I think he's more interested in his job than in women at the moment.'

'Men never give up their interest in women, darling, however interesting the job.'

'Well . . .'

'Is he not playing your game, Marianita? Though how an English accountant could resist your curls and complexion I have no idea.'

'I don't know, *Mamà*. All we talked about was the business – whether it would be a success, whether he and Annabel would ever be able to pay off Oonagh, whether they would take the company to Paris, how much they'd need to expand over the next year if they were to compete on the world market. I had a fine time keeping my eyes open, I can tell you.'

'How can you have been so blind, Marianita? He's obviously in love with Annabel.'

'Oh, I hope not. He didn't talk about her much.'

'Just her business.'

'And that makes him totally infatuated with her? Really, *Mamà*! Maybe he just wants to make a go of the company. Anyway, if he *is* in love with Annabel he'll grow out of it, won't he? Besides, Annabel and Antonio will eventually get married and then Duncan won't stand a chance, will he?'

'Marianita, haven't you forgotten about the English loyal labrador type? Annabel may be out of the running but that doesn't stop the true English dog from longing from afar. I'd forget it if I were you, darling. Now, try and get some sleep. It must be nearly dawn there.'

'Yes, *Mamà*.'

'Give my love to Antonio and remind him it's his father's birthday next week. If he wants his allowance he should try not to forget it.'

'Yes, *Mamà*.'

'Night night, darling.'

Waiting for the dawn, Duncan sat in his springy armchair staring out at the night. *The Brothers Karamazov* lay abandoned in the bathroom. The dishes from his impromptu supper with Mimi were piled in the kitchen sink. Duncan's mind held only one thought: what on earth lay in the flat across the road that could have attracted Antonio, Gladstone, Kenneth and Jean-Luc all within a few days? Even as he stared Gladstone and Antonio came out of that same door. They performed a little private show for Duncan, spotlit by the street light, laughing, slapping each other on the back, shaking hands and then marching off in opposite directions. All Duncan could think about was how sad it was for Annabel to spend the night of her triumph alone while her boyfriend lurked in a tart's boudoir with the unsavoury Gladstone for company.

PART 2

Milan

Chapter 4

THREE days later the London fashion week was over and the general exodus from London to Milan began. Mimi and Annabel were among the first to go, taking the opportunity for a little R&R before the hordes arrived. On the evening of the first day Mimi lounged in her room at the Palace Hotel talking on the phone while she flipped through the mail and messages and the schedule of the fashion shows which would take place over the following week.

'Annabel, this is ridiculous. They can't have the shows this close together! And knowing how late the Italians always are we'll never have a day which finishes before two in the morning.'

'Don't worry. They always manage somehow. I just hope people find time to come and see my showroom.'

'Of course they will. Anyway, you sold enough in London to cover your next season, didn't you?'

'Officially. But Duncan doesn't know that I smudged

the figures a tiny bit to keep him calm. The production costs are going to be higher than I thought, and I really need to sell some of those cheap and easy pieces if we're going to get through to the next show without running to Mummy.'

'Can't you go elsewhere for backing?'

'Nope. She'd take the original two million back if we did that. She hates the idea that anyone other than she might be able to help. Don't tell Duncan.'

'Wouldn't dream of it. Besides, he's got other things to bother him, hasn't he?'

'What things?'

'He's convinced that . . .' Mimi stopped herself. 'Never mind. He's paranoid, that's all.'

'What, Mimi?'

'Oh, it's ridiculous really.'

'Then it won't matter if you tell me, will it? Besides, however bizarre he's being, there's not much I can do with him until he arrives in time for Saul's opening, is there?'

'No. But really, it's too ridiculous.'

'Mimi – speak to me or I'll never let you make up interviews with me again.'

'Well . . .' Mimi paused and chewed the edge of her Versace invitation thoughtfully. 'Put it this way. Duncan thinks that Antonio, Gladstone, Kenneth and Jean-Luc are hatching some plan.'

'Thanks for being so specific. What kind of plan? And when did he see them talking together? Kenneth hates Gladstone, and there's hardly any love lost between Antonio and Jean-Luc, is there?'

'That's why it's so peculiar that Duncan keeps seeing them following each other in and out of a flat across the road from his house.'

'What?'

'Exactly – what have that group of weirdos got in common in the first place, and why on earth would they want to hang around together?'

'Well, it's easy enough to find out. I'll ask Antonio when he gets here for Saul's opening. I expect he's only there in a desperate attempt to keep the others out of trouble. He's probably only doing it for me.'

'You wish. Well, let me know what his excuse is. I can't wait to hear what he has to say.'

'I can't imagine it's that exciting. I'll put you and Duncan out of your misery as soon as I've spoken to him. I expect Mummy's just having them keep an eye on Kenneth. You know how little she trusts him.'

'Maybe. I'm rather hoping for a more exciting reason than that, though.' Mimi changed the subject. She could hear Annabel's dislike for this new chumminess between Mimi and Duncan beginning to scratch in her voice. 'Got any good presents?' Mimi had received only a single bunch of violets from a secret admirer. Oh for the days when she'd be editor in chief of her own magazine. She hated buying flowers herself for her suite.

'This place looks like a hothouse. You can have some if you like. Most of them are so funereal I thought I'd send them all over to Gloria's room as a token of doom for her future,' laughed Annabel.

'Hmm . . . nice. Are you going to Gianfranco's do tonight?'

'I'm so tired.'

'Oh come on, Annabel. You're the toast of the fashion world. Isn't it time you went and just basked in a bit of glory for once without worrying about your clothes, your show, your sales or even Antonio seeing as he isn't here? Besides, Gianfranco came all the way to your showroom to invite you. Remember that piece in the paper: "like a prize-winning hothouse flower, planted still and confident in her beauty, Annabel French sat and patiently accepted the homage of personalities as diverse as Nina Charles and Gianfranco Desire." It'd be churlish not to go when he probably paid the journalist to go that purple.'

'Ah, and there's the rub, because as you and I know this season's colour is pink. Someone as ahead of her time as they say I am couldn't possibly be seen at a purple event. My dear,' she said in an Anthony Blanche drawl, 'it would be t-t-too t-t-too passé. Anyway, George and the others don't arrive until tomorrow. I haven't got any bodies to follow me and make me look more glorious. You know how necessary it is to arrive with one's court at this kind of function.'

'What have you been reading? Come on, Annabel, don't be such a killjoy. They weren't asked, were they? And who'm I going to go with if you don't come with me? Brilliant young fashion editors are always supposed to turn up at parties with brilliant young fashion designers, with or without their hangers-on. And aren't you dying to see

Saul and Gianfranco together again? Darling, who needs West End musicals when you can go and see those two perform for free? Go on, throw on your best creation and I'll come over and get you. Meet you at the Four Seasons at about seven?'

Annabel sighed, not altogether convinced. 'OK, you've got a deal. I'll get the champagne out and get plastered while I wait for you.'

While Mimi scrunched her hair into a mass of glossy black curls and poured herself into her tiny Prada party dress, Annabel called George at the atelier.

'Packed?'

'Yes, Annabel.'

'You have remembered everything?'

'I hope so.'

'Not good enough, George. Hope won't get you far in this business – or haven't you learnt that yet?'

'No, no. I mean, I'm sure. I wish I had help getting to the airport, though.'

'Don't be wet, George – you know we can't afford to pay anyone else to come to Milan. You should be thrilled at this opportunity. It's not everyone who gets to travel the world on business when they're only an assistant.'

'I know, I know. Please don't be cross with me, Annabel. I'm just nervous about the plane, that's all.'

'Don't be ridiculous, George. You're more likely to suffer a car crash than a plane crash, you know.'

'Perhaps I should take the bus then.'

'Don't be facetious.'

'I'm sorry – I'm just a bit tired.'

'Tired! I'm the one who's tired and stressed. If this all goes wrong then it's me who'll suffer, George – remember that. Just turn up on time and with everything tomorrow and don't let me down, all right?'

'All right.'

'God, I wish I hadn't rung you now.'

'I'm sorry.'

'Well . . .' Annabel put the phone down, poured herself a glass of champagne, put on one of her pink lining material party dresses and did a few shoulder rolls to calm herself down. She perched prettily on the arm of a chair and called Antonio. There was no answer. Furious, she swigged the rest of her drink and went to make up.

When Gianfranco Desire gave a party the whole of Milan knew about it. The fashion press and cognoscenti had descended en masse upon the nerve centre of the Italian luxury markets, and they were all heading for the reception, which was intended to start Milan fashion week with a bang. It took Mimi predictably longer than planned to get from her room at the Palace to Annabel at the Four Seasons. Mimi would have been staying with Annabel at the Four Seasons but as usual she'd thought she'd better do the chic thing and share with the other junior editors at a suitably junior hotel. However, when she'd seen the room and fought with the man at reception and realised that they didn't even have a fax machine that worked, she had changed her mind fast. It wasn't even worth trying the Four Seasons, which she knew any amount of backsheesh wouldn't budge, so she had rushed over to the Palace and demanded her usual room, which had been removed from a disgruntled senior editor at a rival magazine and given to Mimi forthwith.

It was eight fifteen when she finally arrived at the Four Seasons. Having negotiated her way across the fashion battlefield of the hotel lobby, she launched herself into Annabel's room.

'Right.' Mimi threw herself down onto a sofa and took a pose. 'What are we wearing?'

'Hello.' Annabel kissed Mimi and gave her a glass of champagne. 'What do you mean, what are we wearing?'

'Well, I can hardly go out in this tired old Prada now that you're flavour of the month, can I?'

'But I haven't got anything here.'

'Bullshit. I'm sure you've got something.'

'No – only stuff I've made for me.'

'Oh, you're so chic the way you avoid telling me I'm too fat to get into any of your clothes.'

'No you're not. I just don't think we suit the same things, that's all.'

'Stop trying to be kind to me. Why can't you just be straight and cruel? Couldn't we customise something? I mean,' she fingered her pale pink and tangerine mousse-line Prada party dress with distaste, 'this is so finished.'

'Mimi, you're so ahead of your time that that particular dress hasn't even hit the stores yet. It's only because

you're such a treasured customer that you get things so far
ahead. It's hardly finished. The hem's still hot from the
Prada steamer.'

'But haven't you got one of those lovely pink dresses
you whipped up at the last minute out of lining material?
I've been dreaming about those ever since the show.'

'If you insist you can try one on. But it was made for
Pandora, so I don't quite know what it's going to do on
you.'

'If I can get it past my hips, you mean.'

'You said it.'

By the time they finally arrived at Gianfranco's party
Mimi was breathless and a little red in the face on account
of trying to pour her lovely round figure into Pandora's
size six dress and eventually giving up and wearing the
battered old Prada which hadn't even appeared in the
shops yet, and Annabel was pleasantly drunk.

'God, it's so nice to go out with none of the whingeing
hangers-on' she cried as they leapt out of the car and stood
in the heated outdoors waiting to enter the inner sanctum
of the party. First they had to negotiate a formidable
reception line involving not only Gianfranco Desire but a
number of magazine editors, major buyers and Saul
Smytheson, photographer to the stars and boyfriend to
Gianfranco. Saul was most impressive in a gold lamé Mao
suit. Mimi couldn't resist reminding Annabel that only
a few hours earlier she'd been claiming that without
hangers-on she couldn't go anywhere.

'I know. Isn't it lovely to be out alone – hangers-on free

zone – no please, Mummy, will you wipe my bottom for me every five minutes.'

'Who does that?'

'You know, my mother, Antonio, George, Duncan.'

'When did Duncan ever need help wiping his arse?'

'Young Master Goodbody – he's only in this for the glory and eventual financial gain. He does own twenty per cent of the equity, you know.'

'You're turning into one of those spoilt famous people who believe it when everyone tells them they're wonder-ful. You're paying Duncan a pittance for what he does for you, and I would have thought it painfully obvious that he doesn't do this because he hankers after the clothes. He sees this venture as a personal challenge.'

'Oh yeah? Since when are you such an expert? Just because you fancy him. Give up, Mimi – he's in love with me and you know it. Anyway, he still whinges.' Mimi began to get really cross.

'Rubbish – he's trying to teach you to be responsible. Someone has to keep an eye on the money or you'd have gone under months ago. You can be such a bitch some-times.' Annabel blushed, furious. 'Without him you certainly wouldn't be here. You may do all the creative stuff, but who do you think makes that cosy little cocoon you work in possible? No disturbances, the right atmos-phere, kid gloves on, everyone – the designer's here. Have a little humility. If all this fame's going to your head like this you'll find yourself in trouble sooner or later. He'll leave you.'

'He won't.'

'How do you know?'

'I just know. This is a personal crusade for him. I'm not sure who he's trying to impress or why, but he doesn't have to work so hard and he doesn't have to take everything I or anyone else in the atelier says so personally. I didn't ask him to make the business some kind of test for himself. I asked him to do a job for a salary. He shouldn't get so involved. He shouldn't worship me so much. He's put me on a pedestal somewhere and has no idea what I'm really like. And he's old enough to know that if he's really going to make a success of the company then he's got to learn to stand back from it and have some kind of life outside the office. Otherwise how can he have any kind of perspective on what's going on? I'm sorry if I was horrid, and I suppose I do take him for granted, but he does whinge all the time and it is nice not to have him hanging on for once. Concede that point at least. And he may be in love with me, but I'm not in love with him, so I wish he wouldn't be so boring and loyal all the time.'

Mimi was so angry she could hardly speak. Annabel smiled at the other queuers and ignored the fury emanating from Mimi's bouncing curls. They stood dutifully waiting to pass through the hallowed pink marble portals of Gianfranco's palazzo and drank the champagne served by waiters dressed only in loincloths and gold paint off crystal trays lit from beneath by strings of tiny white lights. It wasn't the slightest bit cold waiting as there were huge gas flares all along the drive to keep the guests warm.

Only the chill in the atmosphere between them made Mimi shiver and look down at her feet, hoping that they could put the quarrel behind them and enjoy the party. She hated fights, and in spite of being righteously angry with Annabel she couldn't bear to stay furious.

'I wouldn't tell any environmentalists about this place – talk about wasting energy!' Annabel whispered.

'Darling, I never realised you cared.' Mimi laughed. 'Ooh – watch out!' Saul Smytheson was about to surprise Annabel from behind but his hat, just the thing for keeping a tropical sun off as long as the gold paint didn't melt, got caught up in Annabel's hairdo and the whole greeting went astray.

'Annabel, you might've kept still for me,' he cried, nursing a bruised nose.

'I'm sorry.' The girls tried and failed not to laugh. Saul wasn't to know that they'd have laughed at anything that might wipe away the memory of their argument – and he did look rather comical. The crash had knocked his hat and his wig sideways so that now his hair was hanging lopsided over half his face.

'Here, let me help.' Annabel tried to replace the whole arrangement, which only made things worse.

Mimi couldn't help – she was trying too hard not to pee in her pants. She wondered how long it would take the paparazzi to arrive and catch on to this little moment of disarray. Flash – Gay Smith never missed a trick, and there she was capturing Annabel standing with the wig in one hand and the hat in the other, wondering whether it was

worth trying to replace it all or if she should suggest to
Saul that it was time to admit to the world that he was
completely bald. Nobody ever liked his waist-length wigs
anyway.

As far as Milanese fashion parties go, this one was fairly
typical. Annabel and Mimi were greeted by a sea of fuschia
and scarlet, the season's colours. For once the fashion
world had forsaken their habitual black and even the men
were decked out like a collection of birds of paradise.
Mimi and Annabel hugged themselves secretly. They were
new enough to the scene still to be impressed, and they
would always be amused by the sight of the species *Fashio-
nous maximus* at play.

Parasites lounged around the walls comparing sample
sale bargains.

'I know it's a bit last season, but it is Chanel.'

'Not really your colour though, don't you think?'

'But it's Chanel.'

'Well, in that case . . .'

'And then he said that if he didn't sleep with him he'd
ring up Suzy and tell her about the time he was caught
with his pants down and his nose occupied in someone we
all know's apartment at nine o'clock on a Monday morning.'

'No – well, I heard that even if you had your little man
dye it it wouldn't be right. Giorgio's got a special formula
for the colour and he keeps it in a bank vault in
Switzerland.'

'How ridiculous. As if anyone's going to care next season.'

There was even gossip about Annabel, whose face wasn't quite well known enough to be recognised by everybody.

'I heard it was felt.'

'How'm I going to wear felt? I come out in a muck sweat in anything heavier than linen.'

'Darling, it's for December.'

'I know, but everyone'll be wearing it at the end of August. Did she do a cruise version?'

Meanwhile the real VIPs rushed in briefly, breathed air kisses on the favoured few and departed smartly, leaving behind them a glow of Chanel No. 5 and glitter from their eyes, dresses and occasionally neck ties. Their comments and conversation were much more abrupt – they were too famous to have time for whole sentences. Besides, as most of them had mobile phones clasped to an ear while they dropped these pearls of wisdom it was often difficult to know whether they were talking to the person in front of them or the person at the other end of the phone.

'Fabulous.'

'Tomorrow.'

'Call me.'

'Call my assistant.'

'Darling, I don't know whether I'm alive or dead and we're only in Milan!'

'Lunch?'

'Shoot it.'

'St Barts – November.'

'Not that far ahead.'

'Darling, Gloria's already on next March and that's two seasons ahead.'

'Foolish.'

'Fat! There was butter!'

'Too glittery.'

'Admit.'

'Darling – I took my sunglasses off for her!'

A sad, drunk, B list designer sat in one corner with a sad, drunk, B list actor. Saul – positively the star of the night due to his long awaited exhibition opening the following evening and brand-new status as boyfriend of the host – looked upon the pathetic duo and commented: 'I wouldn't go near either of those two with an open flame.'

Annabel and Mimi were treated as stars too. Annabel's collection had been the kind of hit that inspired even *Women's Wear Daily* to wax lyrical, making foolish predictions and suggesting that she was Britain's long awaited answer to Elsa Schiaparelli. Mimi held onto her old friend and new protégée like a leech and they were flirted with, courted, plied with very little drink but every kind of drug available in Milan that evening, and eventually retired exhausted but warmed enough by the admiration to know that they'd survive the next three weeks of fashion mayhem and come out the other side still sane and probably richer.

Duncan, Kenneth, Oonagh, Gladstone and even Antonio were far from their thoughts as they drifted off to sleep on the pair of sofas in the sitting room of Annabel's suite, and when the phone rang neither of them was sure where she was or who was likely to be calling at that time of night.

'Annabel. Darling, is that you?'

'Mmmm . . .'

'Wake up, darling. It's your mother.'

'I know, Mummy.' Annabel reached for her watch discarded on the floor. 'Mummy! It's four in the morning.'

'So? This is important.'

'What is?'

'Kenneth is being sucked into something really nasty by that Jean-Luc de la Grande Bechind and you've got to help me get him out of it.'

'I thought you always relied on Gladstone to keep an eye on those two.'

'This time it's serious and Gladstone doesn't believe me. It's really too much. And I tried to persuade Antonio to investigate, and he told me that Jean-Luc was harmless and I wasn't to worry. What am I to do?'

'Mummy, when are you going to realise that Jean-Luc *is* harmless? I mean, better the devil you know, don't you think? And what kind of really awful thing is he dragging Kenneth into? How do you know about this?'

'Kenneth won't speak to me.'

'So – what else is new?'

'No – really won't speak to me. You know how he's always under my feet and not speaking to me? Well, now I hardly see him. He doesn't come to beg me for money in the mornings. He doesn't shout at me about my being overweight. He doesn't even make me tell him that secretly I can't imagine anything more glorious than sleeping with Jean-Luc too.'

'That's because you're in Paris and he's in London, Mummy. And this has only been going on for one day. He'll be here when you get to Milan tomorrow. Can you really not live without him for one day?'

'But why isn't he here in Paris with me? It's the first time he's ever left me.'

'Perhaps he's getting his own back for being left by you until he was eighteen and pretty enough to be shown off in a Paris drawing room.'

'Darling, don't be horrid. I had to leave you both in England for your own sakes and for your education. I mean, where would an international baccalaureate have got you?'

'Exactly where we are now, I expect. Mummy, I'm not going to go into this now, but you only let us come anywhere near you once Nanny Palls was dead.'

'Are you telling me she didn't look after you well?'

'No, Mummy. You're running off at all sorts of tangents. The fact is that you didn't see us at all for our entire childhoods and so you've only had your beloved Kenneth at your beck and call for five years, so stop pretending that now he's not there it's the end of the world.'

'But we've got used to each other. We need each other. I mean, I have to suffer every day now you insist on being independent, but Kenneth understood that I needed one of you. I'm an old lady now. I need looking after.'

'You're a little over forty, Mummy – that hardly qualifies you for an OAP rail card. Where's Gladstone? Surely he's there at least?'

'No, darling. He's deserted me too. Am I a sinking ship and are they the rats?'

'Rats they certainly are, Mummy. What's Gladstone up to if he's not with you?'

'Oh, some silly story about setting up an exhibition in London and needing a couple of days more to do it in.'

'So why didn't you stay too?'

'I can't leave Madame de Pompadour for so long, can I? And these silly English immigration laws let in all sorts of riffraff but never dogs, not even for a matter of days. She'd have died without me.'

'Mummy, she's a Pekinese, not a person. You could have stayed in London if you wanted to.'

'But they didn't want me,' Oonagh cried.

'Perhaps Gladstone and Kenneth need a break sometimes. Gladstone's been with you constantly for years, and you've had Kenneth with you every day since you welcomed us back into your bosom.' Annabel had a brainwave. 'I expect Gladstone is keeping an eye on Kenneth for you while pretending he's got to do this exhibition thing. And Kenneth grew up in London – I expect he's just catching up with old friends. You'll see him tomorrow.' Annabel wondered if she'd gone over the top. Everyone knew that Kenneth had no friends except for the unsavoury Jean-Luc. She waited for her mother to object. All she heard was weeping down the telephone. She hoped that Oonagh wasn't using Madame de Pompadour to wipe her eyes on – the unfortunate habit always gave her an allergy.

'Mummy, listen to me. There's nothing sinister in Kenneth staying in London for one more day. He's having a break.' Annabel was becoming not a little exasperated. 'Besides, you're all coming to Saul's opening tomorrow night, so you can see him there. Perhaps at last he's cutting those apron strings which have tied him to you all his adult life and is trying out his independence. Don't you think that's healthy, Mummy?'

'Of course I don't. Men always adore their mothers and would rather be with them than anyone else. He's shown me that in so many ways – Jean-Luc especially.'

'Jean-Luc?'

'Yes, darling. Well, in order not to offend me by bringing home another woman he's just got a special man friend. Unfortunately this particular friend is now taking him away from me in just the same way a woman would.'

'Mummy, really. It's four in the morning. This is evidently not a crisis and we can talk about it tomorrow at Saul's. Can't you take some sleeping pills and leave us all alone at least until the sun's up?'

'How was Gianfranco's?'

'Mummy, go to sleep, please?'

'Oh, must I?'

'Yes. I'm going to sleep. Mimi's slept through this

entire conversation. The whole of Europe's asleep. You know how you like to be part of a trend. Well, the trend at four in the morning is to sleep, so why don't you join in with the rest of us?'

'*Ahead* of a trend, darling! Ahead of everything. And you wait and see. I'm not mistaken. There is a plot being hatched and I'm being kept out of it. You mark my words, my girl, if we don't keep our wits about us we'll all be dead in the morning.'

The phone went dead and Annabel sank back into the depths of the sofa and asked a recumbent and snoring Mimi, 'And run over by a bus in the afternoon. What is she on?' before passing out again and forgetting that the conversation had ever happened.

And in London Kenneth was giving Gladstone, Antonio and Jean-Luc a murder lesson. Gladstone was right; Kenneth loved nothing so much as an audience. Gladstone and Antonio still didn't believe for one moment that Kenneth would succeed in killing Oonagh, so they saw no harm in encouraging him.

This session was taking place in the antiseptic emptiness of Antonio's Royal Avenue drawing room. They'd given up using his other girlfriend's flat in Shepherd Market now that they knew that Duncan lived across the street. It wouldn't do for him to see them going in and out of that little door ever again.

Antonio's mind marched up and down the room, not concentrating on Oonagh's carefully arranged demise but on how to persuade Duncan that he shouldn't rat on him to Annabel. Would a little man-to-man talk work? After all, he must understand that a man couldn't be expected to be monogamous, especially when his official girlfriend was one with as little sexual imagination as Annabel. But then Antonio knew in his heart of hearts that Duncan was deeply in love with Annabel and that his loyalties would always lie with her.

Antonio forced himself to concentrate on the matter in hand. The problem posed by Duncan would just have to wait. He went and sat with Jean-Luc and Gladstone on the white leather sofa. Facing them, across an expanse of glass coffee table covered in expensive books of black-and-white photography, sat Kenneth, eyeing the syringe he held before him with a mixture of fascination and anxiety.

'What's in it?' asked Gladstone.

'Insulin,' Kenneth announced with the pride of a man who'd discovered something nearly as exciting as the theory of relativity.

'And?' Antonio sounded bored.

'I'll kill Mummy with it.'

'But she's diabetic already. Insulin won't kill her.'

'It will if I give her triple the dose she should have. This stuff's powerful enough to kill her off in about two minutes flat.'

'Is it just?' Antonio carried on sounding ruthlessly bored even if he was secretly a tiny bit impressed that Kenneth had got this far with his research.

'So you're going to shoot her up with it? When?' Gladstone asked.

'Darling, don't worry about it. We 'ave taken care of all zat side of ze sings,' simpered Jean-Luc, smoothing down his sharp little bob and patting Gladstone's arm.

'Why should I worry? This is nothing to do with me.' Gladstone pushed Jean-Luc away.

'And you're taking it to Milan – through customs?' Antonio asked.

Kenneth's teeth gleamed across the table at Antonio. 'Of course.'

'Isn't that a touch on the dangerous side?'

'Not in the slightest. My mother is diabetic so my need for a syringe is absolutely obvious.'

'Why should you carry around syringes full of uniden- tified substances if your mother is a diabetic? Surely that's her responsibility?'

'Antonio, I would have given you more credit for brains, darling. I carry a syringe full of insulin because I am her dearly beloved son who looks after her as I would my favourite lap dog. I would never go anywhere without the wherewithal to resuscitate her should she go hypogly- caemic on me. The fact that I don't know that this is extra-strong killer insulin is irrelevant. I'll inject her with it and she'll die and it won't be my fault, will it? As for the carriage through customs of this innocuous little sub- stance,' Kenneth held up a masterful hand to stop anyone interrupting him, 'my washbag will be full of the kit that any caring son might need. Not just insulin but sugar solution, lists of medication, prescriptions written in Italian, French and English.' Kenneth grinned at his audience, pleased that he'd made the plan so crystal clear.

Antonio couldn't help interrupting.

'But you've never had anything to do with your mother's diabetes. It's disgusting. Imagine injecting her scrawny little arse.

Or her horrid little tummy or sagging sighs,' added Jean-Luc looking positively ill at the thought.

'Thanks for the contribution, Jean-Luc.' Kenneth turned to Antonio. 'But I am her beloved son who spends most of his time following her around the globe, and everyone thinks I do it because I love her – so it would be perfectly normal for me to carry this sort of kit, wouldn't it?'

Antonio stood and went to the drinks cupboard, the only other piece of furniture in the room apart from a vast stereo system. He poured himself a large vodka and leant back against the cupboard, staring hard at the murderer in training.

Kenneth wilted under his gaze. 'I'll do it, you'll see. Help, Jean-Luc. You explain.' He waved the syringe across the glassy expanse of the table at his lover.

'Darling, do be careful wizz zat' cried Jean-Luc leaping up to plant himself beside Kenneth and deprive him of the murder weapon in one smooth movement. 'Now I know ziss might be difficult for you boys. It is a complicated plan, I know. We've spent months poring over it. But it seemed to us zat ze efficient way to do away wizz ze detested Oonagh was to give her an overdose of her own medicine. Don't you see? Zat way no one will suspect a single sing and we will be 'ome free wizz all 'er moneys and none of 'er aggravation.' Jean-Luc kissed Kenneth and sat back grinning, pleased as punch with his neat summing up of their plan.

'Isn't it brilliant? You are amazing.' Kenneth took Jean-Luc's hand, tears welling up in his eyes. 'I love you, Jean-Luc. You must never leave me. How could I live without you? And Jean-Luc, you know you'll have to help me. You'll have to do it with me. Please, Jean-Luc, promise!'

Antonio looked at Gladstone and laughed. 'You know, they do seem to have planned this well. I'll bet you fifty pounds they actually do it.'

'Nah – they'll never have the balls. And I don't think you've got fifty pounds at the moment, have you?'

'But look at the way they're egging one another on. One of them'll go over the top sooner or later and actually achieve their aim, you know. Give me a moment and I'll be quids in, Gladstone.'

'Never. They're much too pathetic.'

'Don't be mean about us. We are capable of anyssing we put our minds to, aren't we, precious?' Jean-Luc kissed Kenneth.

Gladstone grimaced. 'Do you have to do that in public?'

'Homophobe,' Kenneth spat.

'Fifty pounds it is. Come on, boys, you'd better hand over the money.'

'What money?' Kenneth looked up from chewing his boyfriend's face off, astonished. 'You can't ask us for money.'

'Oh, I think we can. Just a little something to make sure we don't run and tell naughty tales.'

'Tell any tales you like – no one will believe you. Zey will just sink you're jealous, or mad, or probably both.' Jean-Luc began to laugh. 'Imagine, Kenneth – Gladstone turns to Oonagh after she has ravished him for ze fifteenth time zat night and says, "Stop, my darling, your son is going to kill you!" She'll sack you on ze spot for disloyalty and you'll be out on your ear before you can say a single word in your defence.'

'Ha!' Kenneth said triumphantly.

'Fuck,' said Antonio, and poured himself another drink.

'You'll pay, boys,' Gladstone said, his mind churning with ways to persuade Oonagh that she should take more care of her health in future. 'Just you wait and see.' He smiled. 'Now get out before we practise what you've been preaching on either of you!'

Kenneth and Jean-Luc made a speedy getaway, giggling with excitement. Kenneth loved telling secrets and now he had expanded his audience: he could go to Gladstone or Antonio should Jean-Luc ever get bored of listening to his plans. They rushed back to Blakes to consummate their love for each other by watching American gay porn videos and eating pepperoni pizza in the chaos of their room.

Gladstone lay back on the sofa vacated by Kenneth and waited while Antonio got him a beer.

'They're not really going to do it, do you think?' Antonio shouted from the kitchen.

'I dunno. Kenneth sounds really quite keen – and sort of worryingly organised.'

'Yeah, that's the bit that gets me too. I'd never have thought he'd get even this far.'

'I bet it's Jean-Luc who's done all the research.'

'Too lazy. No – I think Kenneth's going to give it a go. It's like he's got something to prove all of a sudden.' Antonio came back with bottles of Becks and bowls of tortilla chips and salsa.

Gladstone sipped his drink thoughtfully. 'So it looks like we have a problem.'

'What do you mean?'

'Well, if Kenneth kills off Oonagh, do you think for a minute he'll give either of us any of the loot?'

'I'll be all right; I'll have Annabel. You, on the other hand, my dear Gladstone, will certainly find yourself out on your ear and having to earn a living all of a sudden.'

'I know. Worrying, isn't it?'

'For you it is.'

'You shouldn't be so smug. Maybe Oonagh's left all the cash to Kenneth, and Annabel will get her business and nothing else.'

'Nah – she wouldn't be so mean.'

'It's possible.'

Antonio sat up and lit a Gauloise. 'OK, let's make a plan. Three things. First of all I have to marry Annabel quickly – don't want her to get distracted by her mother's death or anything. Then at least that avenue will be firmly kept open. Secondly I think you should be prepared to do an exhibition. We might think about Manhattan. You've got some stuff to show, haven't you?' Gladstone nodded. 'Right, well, pad it out a bit and then we'll have an exhibition.'

'I can't organise an exhibition.'

'Ah, but I can. Don't worry about a thing. For a measly twenty-five per cent I'll take the whole thing off your hands.'

'I'll think about it. And what's the third thing?'

'I think we should tell Mimi and see what she thinks about all this.'

'Mimi! She'll panic and have a fit and then everything'll go haywire.'

'She's a cooler customer than she looks, my little sister. You'd be amazed how handy she can be in a crisis.'

'I'll believe it when I see it.'

'I promise. More beer?'

'And bigger women!' Gladstone laughed and reached for another bottle of Becks.

Duncan was worrying what to pack for Milan and wondering if he really had to go. What on earth did a company accountant have to do with Milan fashion week when his company was English and had sold enough to cover another six months without further investment from the company's mother's purse? But Annabel had asked him to go to Milan from a misguided sense of altruism, thinking that if she didn't he'd feel left out, and he was going to Milan because whatever Annabel asked him to do he would. Besides, she might need him. So he stared at the mixture of unsuitable clothes laid out on his crumpled bed. They went rather well with the ancient dark plum velvet cover on the nineteenth-century French bateau lit which had been left to him with the flat by his uncle.

He leant against the Victorian chest of drawers and chewed on a Biro. The clothes looked no better from a distance. He took a slug of claret. They looked no better through alcohol. They represented everything he disliked about himself: old-fashioned, a little frayed at collar and cuffs, and the kind of thing in which one wouldn't be surprised to find neatly sewn name tapes. No wonder Annabel never looked at him if this was the image he projected. He wanted to burn the lot.

For a split second he wished he knew Antonio better – he was always perfectly turned out as a glamorous South American lothario. If only Duncan could achieve that look so effortlessly.

Too proud to call on his boss's boyfriend for advice, he resolved that the following morning on the way to the airport he would stop off at Armani in Bond Street and get them to fit him out with everything he could possibly need for Milan, including a holdall to put it all in. After all, Annabel didn't pay him much, but he didn't have a mortgage and he hardly ever went out in the evenings. His first eight months' salary was sitting barely touched at the Piccadilly branch of Coutts and Co. He might as well splash out with some of it. Besides, he knew that if he were to survive Milan then he needed to arrive with a battledress of Milanese cut and design – no amount of brushing and pressing of his old wardrobe would do.

He went to bed and dreamed of Annabel and Mimi in a confused and disturbing manner which left him sleeping in the wet patch and wondering where his loyalties really lay.

Chapter 5

GEORGE counted again – there were six of the huge black tin trunks known in the business as coffins. Inside them, carefully rolled in reams of tissue paper, was packed the bulk of Annabel's collection. He carried a holdall with accessories and spare silk roses and a pink feather boa which he longed for Annabel to include in the 'look'. The taxi was waiting. He checked again – passport, ticket, money. There was nothing for it but to lock the atelier, go to the airport and get on an aeroplane. For the first time in his life his precious cargo was entirely his responsibility. If only Annabel had let him take along someone from the atelier for extra support. But the budget allowed only for Duncan who had no idea how precious all this baggage was. Well, he did, but George wouldn't trust an accountant with an inch of discarded fabric, let alone Annabel's exquisite collection.

Taking a deep breath he locked the door and watched as

the taxi driver started loading. He'd made a little list of the luggage which he was keeping in the front of his passport, and as each piece was loaded into the taxi he ticked it off. Then he sat gripping the armrest all the way to Heathrow and ticked them off again at the other end. He was supposed to meet Duncan, but there was no sign of him. Not that George would have let him help, but moral support, even from an accountant, was better than nothing. Two trolleys were piled high. How on earth was he to push this lot through to the airline desk? Poor George began to sweat. There was nothing for it. If he was going to force himself onto an aeroplane and get the collection to Milan all on his own he was going to have to give in. He reached into the holdall and draped the fuchsia feathers round his neck. Getting out the false eyelashes and putting them on in the middle of the airport was probably a bad idea: the feather boa would have to do. Courage more or less restored, he forced himself forward at a snail's pace, pushing a trolley with each hand and searching desperately for the British Airways Milan check-in, where they duly refused to let him through because he was three hours early.

'George?' A white-faced and tearful George looked up from his vigil over the luggage.

'Oh, Duncan. Thank goodness you're here. They won't let me on the plane. I got here in plenty of time and then they said I'd have to wait. And they didn't even begin to understand when I told them about the collection. They actually said that they couldn't care less. Can you imagine? I mean, don't these people read the papers? Don't they realise what treasure I'm guarding here?'

'Calm down, George. What did they say when you tried to check in?'

'That I would have to wait my turn. What are we going to do?' It was only at this point that the hapless George noticed that Duncan was dressed in an immaculate spring-weight navy wool suit with a camel overcoat slung much too nonchalantly over his shoulders and that he was carrying an Armani bag bulging with all sorts of secret delights. George blushed. 'Duncan – what's happened to you?'

Duncan screwed up his face and tried to look confident. 'Long story. I'll tell you about it on the plane. Come on. Let's check this lot in.' He took one of the trolleys and started to push it through the crowds towards the correct check-in desk.

George took hold of himself and hurried after Duncan, forgetting in his excitement that he should have checked off all the luggage again before moving it at all and that he'd had no intention of letting Duncan within actual touching distance of the collection, let alone march off with half of it.

Some time later the two men sat next to each other at the front of the economy class cabin of BA flight 206 to Milan. George stroked the feathers of his boa thoughtfully and waited while Duncan shuffled about, trying to fold his legs into the space provided. Not until he was

sure that Duncan was quite settled did George think it
safe to bring up the subject of the dramatic change of
image Duncan had effected overnight.

'So, what's the story with the costume then?'

Duncan grinned. 'I could well ask you the same question.'

'No need, is there? I often wear feather boas.'

'In airports?'

'Why not? I always find that a little armour goes a long
way.'

'Are you that frightened of flying?'

'I'll tell you when we land. I've never done it before. I
haven't done much travelling, you see. I went to Boulogne
once on a school trip but that was on a boat and that was
nerve-wracking enough. I was sick the whole way.'
George batted his real eyelashes at Duncan before he
could stop himself. 'More sensitive than I look, I am.'

Duncan chuckled 'I wouldn't bother flirting with me,
George. Even with the wardrobe turnaround I'm still the
same person.' He ran one hand through his crumpled hair
and pushed his glasses up his nose with the other.

'Wouldn't dream of it, darling.' George laughed.
'You're hardly my type, are you?'

Duncan decided to change the subject. 'How was your
date with Rory Williams the other night?'

'You noticed he asked me out? Ooh lovey, there's more
to you than meets the eye, isn't there? I thought you were
glued to your computer and never noticed what we creatives get up to. Well, if you must know, it was mos

unsatisfactory. He's older than he lets on, you know, and his tastes are dead old-fashioned.'

'Really?'

George warmed to his subject. 'I mean, you'd have thought the style director of such a huge magazine would be a bit more modern in his outlook, but he took me to the Room at the Halcyon and we were surrounded by ageing rock stars who he insisted on snogging all night, and he made me eat much too much and then put me in a taxi and sent me home.'

'Sounds like a perfectly good evening. Perhaps I should go out with him instead. Good food and an early night are just my kind of thing.'

'Well, they're not mine. All that foie gras and star fuck-ing – and all for nothing if he insists on being in bed by midnight. Perhaps he turns into a pumpkin if you keep him out too late.'

'I'd say anything was possible with Rory.'

'Well . . .' George looked at Duncan. 'But you've taken me off my chosen subject of the flight. What brought about this dramatic change of image and how on earth did you do it?'

It was Duncan's turn to pause. He stared at the seat back in front of him and thought for a moment. Why had he done it?

'I suppose . . .' he began slowly. 'I suppose that I think his trip to Milan is important and there's a lot of work to be done, and I don't want to worry about my ancient patched tweed jackets looking out of place.'

'And? That's hardly enough to persuade you to go to Armani for the morning. I'm impressed. With the greatest respect I wouldn't have thought you'd know the difference between Armani and Marks and Spencer.'

Duncan sighed. 'You get better advice at Armani. Besides, Annabel would – know the difference.'

'Oh, that's it then. Truth will always out darling, especially when I'm wheedling it from its hidey hole.' George grinned from ear to ear. 'You're chercheing la femme, aren't you? I always wondered why you did this job. Obviously you can hardly be in it for the money – none of us is. I'm in it for the glory of being Annabel's assistant and right-hand booby. When she gets snapped up by some huge French house to design for them I'll be there to look after her business at home for her.' He looked at Duncan with new interest. 'And you're in love with her.' George was so absorbed with this idea that he hadn't even noticed that they'd taken off and only realised it when an air stewardess offered him a drink.

'Ooh!' he breathed nervously and shot a questioning look at Duncan. 'I don't suppose it's on expenses, is it?'

Duncan was relieved to find such an instant change of subject at his elbow. 'I think you'll find it's free.'

'Free! Oh, in that case I'll have a Bloody Mary. It'll clash beautifully with my feathers.'

The stewardess laughed and handed over the drinks: Bloody Mary and what George would have called 'a bloody predictable gin and tonic' for Duncan, who would have hated George to realise that he needed to steady his nerves as much as George did.

'Think you'll ever get anywhere with her?'

'What ?'

'Annabel. Do you think you'll ever get near her?'

Duncan stared straight ahead and frowned. 'No.'

'Well, you may be brilliant but you can hardly compete in the looks department with that Antonio, now can you?'

'I don't think she's got much time for my sort. Apparently her family call me the Neanderthal man. I know I look like a prop forward but I'm not that thumping on the eye, am I?'

'More of a winger, I'd say, fleet of foot and useful in an emergency.'

'Thanks. I didn't have you down as a rugby expert.'

'What? Are you seriously suggesting that I ignore all those gorgeous men?'

'Not the forwards.'

'No, darling, I told you – those lovely boys on the wing.'

'Easy, tiger.'

'Oh calm down, Duncan. Why Annabel, though? I'd have thought she'd be a bit ice maiden for you. Too much frost in the mornings doesn't make Jack a happy boy, you know.'

'I admire her. I don't know much about the clothes side of things but I think she's brave and gutsy and determined and clever.'

'Perfect wife and mother material.'

'Who says that's what I want?'

'Yeah — you really want to spend the rest of your life with a career woman who'll only use you to check the accounts once a quarter. No, you don't want her. I mean, I know she's my boss and everything so I should be more loyal, but you look like the kind of man who'd need a bit of warmth in his life.'

'She's not that icy. She just works hard, don't you think?'

'Ever seen her do a Nescafé Frappé on me?'

'Nope.'

'And I thought you were so beady-eyed, Duncan. Watch out for it then. It's iced coffee with a barbed wire froth. You should try it some time. What about that Mimi?'

'Mimi?'

'Yes, Mimi. Now she'd fire up anyone prepared to give her a go. I bet her bedroom isn't all cold silver walls and brass rails. Nor her underwear either. No — I think you should look more in her direction.'

'This sounds like a conspiracy. Did Annabel tell you to talk to me about this?'

''Course not. She loves having all the attention, even if she has no intention of giving anything back. Don't be so touchy. I'm just good at playing Cupid, that's all, and I can always tell when someone's pointing their arrow in the wrong direction. You'll never get anywhere with Annabel.'

'It'll be so sad if she ends up with Antonio. He's disgusting.'

'She, my poor blind friend, will end up with no one. She goes out with Antonio because she ought to go out with someone and for no other reason. She may complain that he's not there for her all the time and he doesn't support her enough and all that crap, but frankly she's avoiding commitment and waiting till she's old enough for the pressure to be off. Then she'll sink into happy solitude and spend the rest of her life becoming more and more wrapped up in herself.'

'You really think so? That's tragic.'

'No, it's not. She'll be happy; Antonio will be happy when she drops him because then he can go round picking up underage tarts. He'll miss the money, of course, but you can't have everything.'

'Underage tarts!'

'He's just like his father, you know. Can't keep his hands off anything in a skirt under the age of sixteen.'

'How do you know all this stuff?'

'I'm a nosey old cow, that's why. And an expert on human nature. You mark my words – watch that Mimi and forget Annabel.'

'Interesting theory, but I'm not sure I'll act on it.'

'Then you're a bigger fool than I took you for.'

Annabel had originally planned on setting out her wares to be sold in a small boutique just outside the Fiera Milano, the centre for most of the fashion shows, but her success in London meant that she'd been offered one end of the gallery where Saul Smytheson was to have the opening of his photography exhibition that evening. She sat on a plastic chair in the empty space watching the hysteria at Saul's end of the premises and waiting for her own show to arrive.

'Not there, you idiot.' Saul sounded just like Oonagh ordering Kenneth about. 'How many times do I have to tell you that the Morgan/Pandora pictures take pride of place on that wall? Does *anyone* here have any artistic sense?' He smoothed his sugar-pink shantung drawstring pants and pointed furiously at the team of people working for him. 'My God! I've seen worse done by my decorator and we all know what kind of a baboon he is.' Saul turned and caught sight of Annabel watching from her empty corner. 'Annabel, darling, help! I can't do this on my own and your people seem to have deserted you. Help me hang these things, please.'

Against her better instincts Annabel went towards him. Until the boys arrived there was nothing for her to do, and she had no intention of going to any of the Milan fashion shows – she'd seen enough in London and needed a break. She'd be supportive of the other British designers in Paris the following week. Luckily that season no Brits were showing in Milan so she could avoid the shows for a few more days. Besides, she knew she wouldn't have to do much for Saul – he wouldn't let her. He just needed an audience if he was to get any work done.

'Now. listen everybody, we have an artist here. Let's not disappoint her, shall we?'

'Ooh, look at her – all revved up and only old places to go.' Annabel turned to find Saul's erstwhile boyfriend

Bobby Frisco wobbling his way into the gallery. This was all they needed.

'Hello, Bobby.'

'Ooh, love, what are you doing hanging around this past-it queen? I thought you were much more up to the minute than that. Look – only pictures of that Max Fyodov to hang. You know they're almost a year old. Quite finished, I'd say. And all for the love of a White Russian who's not interested.'

Saul had turned an unattractive shade of grey with green touches at throat and wrist. 'Get him out of here,' he spat. 'He's a wicked little boil on the arsehole of humanity and obviously needs more vicious lancing than I thought I'd already given him.' Saul advanced on the unsteady-looking Bobby who pulled himself upright from his leaning position by a stack of pictures.

'Keep your knickers on, Sauly – no need to get so antsy. I'm off.' Bobby weaved his way towards the exit and turned, holding onto the door handle for support. 'But I'll be back, don't you worry. And don't you forget it.' And he was gone.

Annabel turned back to Saul to find him shaking and obviously incapable of hanging anything. She sat him on the chair she'd occupied earlier and let the picture hangers get on with their work. They had a plan made up for them by Saul and so couldn't go too wrong. She went to comfort him.

'Oh Saul, you must be shaken. Look, your wig's all awry.'

'I'm not shaken, just slightly stirred.' Saul straightened

his wig determinedly. 'Who on earth paid for that little rat to come all the way here from Manhattan? Someone must really hate me.'

'Never mind who's paying his way. You've got an exhibition opening this evening. Come on, the hangers know what they're doing. Let's go back to the Four Seasons and get you a drink.'

'No. I won't let my past ruin my future.' Saul stared at the floor and tried to get the strength together to stand up. He didn't have time.

'Darlings — it's all right. I'm here now.'

Oonagh had arrived. She kissed Saul and Annabel and moved in a predatory manner towards the workmen.

'Mummy, you don't have to kiss them. They're workmen. I don't think they'd appreciate it.'

'Don't be ridiculous. Everyone gets kissed in Italy.'

'Oh my God.' Annabel blanched. 'She's drunk already.'

'She's always drunk at this time of the day.' Saul looked fondly at Oonagh. 'You can tell the time by her. Let her kiss the workmen. They might find it amusing.'

'Or die from the fumes.'

'You should love your mother more, dear. She's only here to help, you know.'

'On no she isn't. She's here to be photographed by all the magazines. Why else do you think she went back to Paris between leaving London and coming here? You don't imagine she'd allow anyone but her beloved Phillipe to do her hair. She never washes it, you know — just puts a can of dry shampoo on it every day she's away from Paris and has

Gladstone hoover the evidence from her shoulders on an hourly basis.' Annabel sat down, pout firmly in place, on the chair vacated by Saul who'd had a sudden surge of energy now that his audience had doubled.

Suddenly the gallery became the happening place it was supposed to be. The season's pink was more than just a theme – it was the only colour in evidence. The florists arrived with the arrangements for the evening; all the pink and red roses they'd been able to get hold of were jammed into huge wicker baskets and balanced precariously on antique church candlesticks. There were more baskets of rose petals which would be scattered over the floor just before the party began. The caterers arrived and made rose-shaped tables with rose-coloured food spread over the tablecloths made of gold-spattered canvas. There were pink macaroons, shrimps, cranberry juice and vodka jellies; and the wine merchant arranged pink bins around the feet of the flowers into which the pink champagne and ice were to be stuffed just as the first guests arrived. There were even a couple of male models dressed as cupids posing by the door with a *livre d'or* for the guests to sign. They also had a list detailing those who'd been invited, those who'd be allowed in anyway and those who weren't under any circumstances to be allowed to darken the doors of the gallery, especially Bobby Frisco. Even Annabel had to admit that the decor was pretty, especially the boys. They wore wings and bows and arrows, and crosses hung from their pierced nipples. Someone had sprayed their shoulders with gold, and as they wandered round the gallery admiring the photographs they left a little trail of glitter for those who admired them to follow.

Annabel even found, with uncharacteristic generosity of spirit, that Saul's huge framed prints of trademark bright exposure featuring every celebrity of the past few years were not as awful as she'd imagined they would be. She eyed the miniature pink macaroons and watched as her mother hindered the works by rearranging everything. An assistant followed Oonagh around and moved everything back to their original positions once she'd passed.

'Darling, it's heaven,' Oonagh gushed to Saul. 'And wherever did you come up with this divine pink?'

'It is new, isn't it?'

'New! It's positively twenty-first century. And your little cupids are so dreamy. You could have a little game for them; I could be a lucky winner and take one home.'

'Darling, I've paid for them to work for me all night. I'm afraid they're mine.'

'Well, if Gladstone never turns up I might just have to steal one to keep me warm for the night.'

Oonagh and Saul's fawning over one another was ignored by Annabel. She was staring at the naked walls of the corner where her collection was to hang. There was no sign of Duncan or George with the clothes, Mimi was busy being a junior fashion editor and cramming as many shows as she could into her schedule and Antonio, natch, wasn't due to arrive until the party actually started. Annabel was becoming increasingly irritated. The stuffed mannequins with china faces like Victorian dolls which she'd ordered to be delivered hadn't arrived and she couldn't even think how to solve that problem. If she'd known herself a little better she'd have realised that she too needed an audience in order to achieve anything, and that her mother was not enough of an audience to get her going. She sat, lost, on her orange plastic chair and watched as the minute hand on her watch crawled towards the next hour. She felt useless and could think of nothing but to try and call Duncan on his mobile and see if he'd arrived yet. Stuff the cost, where was George? No answer.

'Now darling – have a glass of champagne and stop moping. When are you going to do something about your little corner and cheer it up? You can't let Sauly down by not pulling your weight, you know.'

'Thanks for the advice, Mummy. I'm waiting for the boys to turn up with all the kit.'

'Well, wait any longer and the party'll be over.'

'Thanks for the reminder.' Annabel took the glass handed to her by her mother, who was leaning precariously against a pillar. Annabel briefly imagined tying Oonagh to the pillar for the evening for her own safety and took a deep swig of her drink. 'Talking of missing luggage, where's Gladstone?'

'As if I could care, darling. I've hardly spoken to the little rat since he left me in London.'

'You left him, Mummy. You went to Paris.'

'Well, I think he should have a few days in the Antarctic of my outer circle before I even consider letting him near me again. I know Kenneth needs looking after, but in that case they should all have come back to Paris with me.'

'They are not your court, you know, Mummy,' Annabel scolded.

'They may as well be, the amount I pay them.'

'Do you have any friends that aren't in it for the money?'

'Why should I? Thanks to my generosity the ones I have will never leave me. I'm secure with them.'

'Don't you worry about there being a coup?'

'What? Kenneth taking over the citadel of the Champs de Mars in the middle of the night? He wouldn't have the initiative.'

'You are charming the way you support your son and heir.'

'Realistic, rather.'

'With any luck he's disappeared for good,' muttered Annabel.

'Darling, there's no need to be bitchy. He is your brother after all.'

'Aren't I the lucky one? Duncan – at last! Where've you been?'

Duncan strode up, his hair more than usually rumpled. 'Held up at the airport. Sorry we're late. Is everything OK?'

'No. Where's George?'

'Bringing the luggage. He won't let me touch it. Says it has to be counted through his hands and his hands alone or we're bound to lose all of it.'

'Honestly, that boy had better grow up or I'll have to

replace him.' Annabel stormed out to the street where George was battling with the coffins and trying to stop the feather boa from getting in the way. The Milanese taxi driver was getting increasingly irritated with this fool's refusal to pay until every piece of luggage was installed inside the gallery.

'George, for God's sake get a move on,' Annabel snapped. 'And take that frightened rabbit look off your face – it clashes with that stupid feather boa.'

Duncan stood ignored in the empty end of the gallery and looked miserable. Annabel had showed absolutely no sign of noticing the navy Armani suit and nobody else even cared that he was there. Perhaps he should chuck in this stupid industry and go home. He looked around him at the minions sowing rose petals beneath the photographs and shrugged. He'd better get back to the hotel. If he'd spent all this money on clothes he may as well wear some of them for the party.

Room 43 at the Four Seasons was a mess. Kenneth and Jean-Luc had spread over every available surface everything they'd brought with them to Milan and were fighting over who was to wear what to the party.

'But the pink Gucci pants suit me better, Jean-Luc. I hate to be bitchy, but have you really got the arse for them?'

'Arse to you too. Of course I 'ave ze arse for zem. I bought zem, didn't I? Darling, you can't wear zem anyway. You told me you wanted to wear ze lemon-yellow Nehru

jacket wizz ze lime-green paper taffeta pants you stole off
Pandora Williams the last time you went rifling through
her Uncle Rory's wardrobe.'

'But I was lying. Yellow's so finished. You know what
it's like in Milan. If you wear a different colour from
everyone else nobody talks to you.'

'Why don't you pretend to be a fashion editor and wear
ze black velvet? Look – I even 'elp you wizz ze Peter Pan
collar.'

'But I'm bored of looking like Little Lord Fauntleroy.'

'But you are a little lord, aren't you, my lovely?' Jean-
Luc snaked his way across the floor holding out an
exquisite black silk velvet suit with plus fours and beautiful patent leather dancing shoes to match. 'I love you
when you wear ziss. You are beautiful. I want you in it.
Really.'

Kenneth wasn't to be seduced. 'But I look about five
years old in it. Anyway, I'm the big star of the evening. I'm
the one who has to murder my mother. If you want me to
kill her so you can get your hands on all that lovely money
then you have to let me wear what I want!'

'Oh murder schmurder. You must still be beautiful.
You can wear ze black velvet. You must look ze part a
little. What murderer do you know who wears pink velvet
Gucci *pantalons*?'

'I'll set a trend then. Where does it say that you have to
wear black velvet pedal pants to murder people? We don't
know any murderers. They hardly do features on them in
the better magazines, do they?'

'Oh – wear ze black. Look, it 'as a little pocket for ze syringe. It is too neat, no?'

'No.'

'Please.'

'No.'

'Pretty please?'

'With your English you can come up with something better than pretty please, surely?' Kenneth picked up the Gucci trousers and began to put them on. He was already wearing lilac silk socks and a lilac and pink checked silk shirt to go with them. In all cases he would wear the yellow grosgrain tie, and the fuchsia Gucci jacket was laid out on the back of the sofa ready with a pair of lime-green kid gloves and a scarlet satin handkerchief in the breast pocket. He was not going to change his mind. Like George he needed armour to get his job done, and not even Jean-Luc was going to detract him from his mission. Unless . . . Jean-Luc had dropped to his knees before Kenneth and bowed to kiss the lilac silk-covered toes. Before Kenneth had time to snap shut the flies of the trousers Jean-Luc had got there first.

'Not even this kind of pretty please?'

'No, Jean-Luc – not now. I've got to get into character.'

'What do you mean?'

'Well, I'm hardly a natural murderer, am I? If I'm going to centre my energy sufficiently to carry out matricide in front of an audience of all the people I most admire then I need to save my strength. I'm in training. No sportsman ever indulges in fellatio five minutes before a match, do they? Well, I'm the same. And I'll bloody well wear the Gucci. If you're so fond of the black velvet then wear it yourself.'

'Kenneth! What's got into you?'

'I've found my vocation and I'm not going to let you boss me around any more.'

'Look, just because you marched through customs without being stopped doesn't make you an expert at murder yet.'

'You wait. I'm without fear.'

'Bullshit.' Jean-Luc was nervous enough to forget his French accent and fey language. 'Who the hell do you think you are, Kenneth? You'd be nobody without me. I'm the only friend you have, the only lover you've ever had apart from a series of scrofulous youths at that prehistoric school you went to, and I'm the only person who can protect you from your mother. I made you.'

'How *dare* you speak to me like that?' Kenneth screamed. 'You may have done all those things, but never forget that I'm doing the killing here and that gives me a power and an experience which you'll never have. And you may have made me but I paid for you to do it. Without me you'd still be waiting tables in that horrid bar in Pigalle. So just be careful what you say, Jean-Luc.'

'What? Where does all this come from?'

'You say you made me? Well, this is what you've created and if you don't like it then you can go fuck yourself for all I care.'

Kenneth marched, silk socked and shirted, into the bathroom and slammed the door. Jean-Luc collapsed onto the sofa, stunned by the metamorphosis of Kenneth into a real-life killing machine. He grabbed the whisky he'd been drinking and swallowed it all in one go. If Kenneth was going to force him to do the Little Lord Fauntleroy act then he'd need a double of Scotch courage. He got up to pour himself another.

'Aren't we nervous,' Kenneth spat on exiting the bathroom. He began a careful arrangement of clothes and accessories about his person. 'You should be careful, sweetie, or I might start practising on you.'

'Mimi, it's taken forever for us to find you.'

'Don't you ever knock?'

'You should lock your door, darling – you never know who might burst in on you.' Gladstone and Antonio threw themselves down on Mimi's bed and watched her wriggle into her Prada party dress, freshly cleaned and pressed for Saul's opening.

'You look lovely in that. Where did you get it from?' Antonio asked.

'Antonio! What do you want?'

'Just to catch up. Can we come to the party with you?'

'Hadn't you better go with your official significant others?'

'Annabel's storming around the gallery and shouting at George, and Oonagh's there just making things worse. We thought we'd go with you instead. Come on, Mimi –

don't you want to arrive at the party of the season with two dreamy men on your arms?'

Mimi couldn't help laughing. 'All right, all right. Go and find something to drink in the fridge and get me a glass of it and wait while I do my hair.'

Antonio pranced towards the bar patting his sister playfully on the bottom in passing. 'You really do look lovely, you know.'

She hit him affectionately. 'Get me that drink and watch the compliments – I might start taking you seriously and get thoroughly big-headed.'

'No, you can't. Your hair's big enough as it is – you won't get through doors if your head grows any larger!' Antonio opened three beers, poured Mimi's into a glass and gave Gladstone his still bottled.

'So . . .' Mimi twisted her hair into a chignon and started shoving hundreds of pins into it in the vain hope that it might stay in place. 'What's the news?'

'Well, Kenneth and Jean-Luc are planning on killing Oonagh.'

'*What?*' Mimi forgot her hair and sat on the end of her bed looking in stunned amazement at her brother and Gladstone.

'Yes, sir,' Gladstone laughed. 'Kenneth says he's going to kill Oonagh and take all her money and make us all destitute.'

'You're joking!'

'Well, we're not taking the threat very seriously, are we, Gladstone?' said Antonio.

'Nope. I mean, can you see Kenneth doing anything more aggressive than demanding alterations on a new suit? It'll never happen.'

'But you'd better warn Oonagh.'

'She'd never believe us,' Antonio told her.

'And I wouldn't dare,' added Gladstone. 'She'd throw me out on my ear for being disloyal.'

'Not before time,' Mimi pointed out.

'Don't be mean. We get on very well together.'

'Rubbish! She's twice your age and you think she's ridiculous.'

'Pitfall of the job, I'm afraid,' said Antonio. 'Our friend here is a professional gigolo. He takes his work much too seriously to let the fact that he doesn't actually like his rich paramour very much get in the way of his unarguable success.'

'Shut up, Antonio. I'm only doing this till I've got enough together to do an exhibition and then I'll make my fortune and become an honest lover to someone my own age.'

'Bullshit! You'll never do it.'

'Stop it, you two,' snapped Mimi. 'You announce calm as a pair of iced cucumbers that Kenneth's threatening matricide and then find time to argue about what Gladstone does for a living. We've got to do something.'

'Oh calm down, Mimi. We'll keep an eye on her. Don't worry – we won't let her out of our sights.'

'So what are you doing here?'

'Well, she's safe now, isn't she? She's at the gallery getting drunk.'

'So if I were you I'd get over there now and keep an eye on her.'

'Come on then. Stop gassing and get your lipstick on and we can all go.'

'I'm going to do something about this.' Mimi shoved one final pin in her hair – watched the whole arrangement fall down, shrugged and grabbed her Gucci faux Mongolian lamb coat.

'You can't wear that!' Antonio was shocked.

'Why not?'

'It ruins the line. Come on, we'll keep you warm getting there. Honestly, you'd never think you were a fashion editor.'

'And I'm not convinced you two are telling the truth about this Kenneth murdering Oonagh business.'

'Well, as he'll never do it there's no need to worry about that, is there?' Antonio said soothingly.

'Keep an eye on him, boys, won't you? We don't need any nasty accidents to take our attention off the collection, do we?'

'Your chance to photograph Annabel's collection in Paris, you mean.'

'Don't be nit-picky, Antonio.'

'Wouldn't dream of it, darling.'

The party was in full Milanese swing when Jean-Luc and Kenneth finally arrived. The strict hierarchy of the fashion world meant that the star of the show, Saul, held the centre space, and those who mattered circulated within the roomy bubble which surrounded him. The maybes, the nearly theres, the junior fashion editors and other people who'd actually been invited to the opening took up a more crowded space, a further five metres around the inner circle. The true parasites, which is where Jean-Luc and Kenneth belonged, lined the walls like an insulation against the outside world.

However, Kenneth and Jean-Luc had as little time as Oonagh for these social niceties. They headed straight for the inner circle, where Oonagh was attempting to hold court with Antonio and Gladstone as her only audience. None of them took any notice of Annabel, who was being fêted by her fans as they came and went from the party. Annabel's little spot was ideal. People could stop, admire, order even, without ever spending more than a regulation five minutes on the exquisite pieces of her collection. Even old friends and fashion editors never stayed long.

Antonio had barely had time to kiss his girlfriend briefly on the lips before being swept away by Oonagh, who wanted to introduce him to an oil magnate boyfriend of a supermodel who might, should Antonio actually try and talk to him, offer him a job. Oonagh loved Antonio for his looks, but hated the fact that in her gross annual expenditure he featured as a non-tax-deductible luxury in Annabel's accounts. Annabel was so busy being fêted that she hardly noticed that Antonio had arrived and certainly forgot to ask him if he thought Kenneth and Jean-Luc were up to anything stupid.

Duncan did notice Antonio. He noticed everything. He sat behind a table taking the orders and trying not to look too flabbergasted by the passing throng. He couldn't believe that there was not one person there not wearing scarlet or fuchsia. Even Annabel, exquisite in one of her lining material party dresses and a pair of perspex and pearl Manolo Blahnick heels, was conforming to that season's convention. Only Jean-Luc, in a perfectly hideous black velvet pageboy suit, wore anything that could be described as original. Duncan found the whole thing blinding and finally understood why everyone wore sunglasses even when the lights were turned down so low.

Duncan himself was sporting an unlikely dark red smoking jacket. The salesman at Armani had done his best to persuade him into a pale moley pink but Duncan had refused with such determination that the man who'd been known to put Gladstone Frith into white rabbit, an expensive disaster that even Oonagh had been forced to admit was ghastly, could get no further than oxblood velvet with this recalcitrant customer. He sat in his corner watching and imagining what he might say should anyone ever speak to him. He wondered if 'No, it's all a bit too fash for me, doll' would go down well and decided that it might only if said by someone like Rory Williams. The style director was dancing round the walls of the exhibition claiming that every photograph except those of his niece, Pandora, was a load of excrement.

'Hello, Duncan.' Duncan jumped. Someone was actually speaking to him.

'Mimi – hi. Shouldn't you be hanging out with the in crowd? You'll lose your job if you're seen with someone as lowly as me.'

'I'd better be careful then. Gloria Wharton might fire me if I'm caught coagulating with an accountant!'

'She might indeed.'

'No, of course she wouldn't. Nobody knows who you are and besides, you might be the star of the party. It's not as if we're surrounded by straight boys. I won't tell anyone if you don't. Otherwise you might find yourself being mobbed by desperate fashion women.'

'Yuck.'

'Not really your kind of thing this, is it? You look thoroughly bored.'

'Mesmerised, you mean. Who are all these people?'

'Never mind that – what a wonderful jacket. Whose is it?'

'Mine.' Duncan looked confused.

'No, darling, who made it? Honestly, I'm going to have to give you some language lessons so that you understand a little more of what's going on around you.'

'I'm not that confused.' He smoothed the lapels of his jacket nervously. 'It's Armani. What do you think? Is it a bit over the top?'

'Over the top! Darling, you're the only person here who could get away without being stared at in the street as if they were some kind of alien.'

'Thanks.' Duncan dried up. Small talk was never his strong suit. 'You look nice,' he managed eventually.

Mimi twirled and giggled. 'It's the nightly outing of my little Prada moment. You know, during the day this dress becomes positively drab and boring, but as soon as the sun sets the colours in it begin to shine. They should have called it the Cinderella dress.'

'Mimi Ytuarte – who are you wearing?' Rory descended upon her, ignoring Duncan, and made her twirl again, his eyes filled with the kind of avarice displayed by Madison Avenue matrons at a Chanel sample sale. 'I do believe you've got that edible little Prada moment, you wicked little girl.'

Mimi tossed her midnight curls and laughed. 'Be nice enough to me and I'll lend it to you, Rory.'

'Oh, love – wouldn't get past my middle-age spread, I'm afraid.' Rory eyed his tiny waist with admiration. 'No, when you get to my age you need something a little more . . . constructive.'

'Who makes your corsets?' Mimi enquired.

'Darling, I've just done a story on him. You know, he has an eighteen-inch waist himself. You should see him in an evening suit, all red satin and starch beneath that soft black wool. I could hardly keep my hands off him.'

'How do you know about the red satin?'

'He wears it over his shirt, of course.'

'Of course, how could I have been so stupid?'

'Well, if your underwear was that beautiful you'd want to show it off too, wouldn't you?'

Duncan, ignored again, sat back in his chair behind the

desk in Annabel's instant boudoir and watched as the circle moved round.

'Nina!'

'Pandora! What have you done to your hair?'

'It's only hairspray dye – what do you think?'

'I think you'd better put a towel over your pillowcase before you sleep on it in case it comes out.'

'Oh you're so practical! Who cares if it comes out? Seems like Diana Vreeland's view of India's here to stay for the season. Bright pink hair can only be just the thing.'

'Wish I had your nerve, darling.'

'No, you don't. You hate it. But don't worry. I promise it won't last.'

Nina laughed at Pandora Williams, the six-foot, usually raven-haired, super darling of the supermodels. 'Nothing in your life ever does.'

'Careful, Nina. I'd hate to think you were being bitchy.'

'Never.'

Duncan was more interested in another cluster of people. He still thought there was something funny going on between Gladstone, Antonio, Kenneth and Jean-Luc, even though there'd been no further evidence of carousing in the flat across the road from his own in Shepherd Market. He watched the patterns they made.

Antonio and Gladstone were never more, never less than three feet from each other and Oonagh. Kenneth looked a little flushed and unusually fiddly. He couldn't leave the arrangement of gloves and handkerchief in his breast pocket alone. And, most peculiar, he wasn't

speaking to Jean-Luc, who stood behind him looking furious, morose, nervous and fidgety all at the same time.
And they too were never more than three feet from
Oonagh. Usually they couldn't wait to get away from her.
Duncan watched, unnoticed, camouflaged by order books
and oxblood velvet, and waited for whatever was to
happen.

'I'm learning to cook.'

'Why?' The non sequiturs of the evening before at
Gianfranco's party continued in their bizzarre arrangements.

'She said it was fabulous.'

'I thought a little too lilac.'

'No, pink.'

'Dull, no?'

'Oh darling, not with the foie gras.'

Duncan watched as Kenneth wiped sweat from his
brow and shifted a few inches nearer his mother. Jean-Luc
pointedly looked away and tried to begin a conversation
with Pandora Williams, who blanked him. She was posing
for Gay Smith in front of a huge blown-up photograph of
herself on a throne in a Moroccan courtyard and didn't
need hangers-on to ruin the line. The babble of conversation continued.

'Of course I didn't eat any.'

'Never, and didn't he say he'd cover it?'

'Cover her, more like.'

'Darling, the bloodlines would be exquisite.'

'Hmm – and the children could launch a perfume.'

'Children! No, buy them.'

'Apparently they're reduced at the Gall Laff.'

Oonagh launched herself at Gloria Wharton, kissing her warmly and ruining her hairdo in one neat move. Kenneth tripped over something and hardly recovered himself. His weasel expression of fear and guilt caused Duncan to stare. Why wasn't he holding Jean-Luc's hand and doing as his boyfriend told him as he usually did? Everyone else was too engrossed in their conversations to take any notice of Kenneth's movements.

'Horrid thought – all those sales girls.'

'Not in the pink jackets.'

'No, orange sari fabric. Too Southall, you know.'

'And on a dog!'

'Well, it doesn't matter what you wear as long as it's Gucci.'

And then the crowd parted and there was a sudden hush. Duncan saw Bobby, the ex-boyfriend of Saul, throw himself into the mêlée having knocked the doormen to the floor. Brandishing a baseball bat, he swung through the crowd like a latter-day Errol Flynn and landed a right-handed swing on the side of Gianfranco Desire's head. And as Gianfranco sank to the floor Duncan saw Oonagh, her mouth open in a scream, sink in formation with him, knocking over an arrangement of roses which came down with her. A horrified hush fell upon the assembled throng. There were rules about how to behave at fashion photographers' openings but none seemed applicable when the stars of the cast started collapsing all over the floor.

Bobby Frisco began to laugh. He sat down heavily on the white painted concrete floor, smearing rose petals over his white moleskins. At least Jean-Luc was no longer the only person not wearing the requisite pink or scarlet. And Kenneth slipped his syringe, which looked like nothing so much as an expensive steel fountain pen, back into his breast pocket and took Jean-Luc's hand, waiting for events to unfold. He held his breath in anticipation and was shocked to find that he had an erection which no amount of attention from his lover would ever give him. His and Bobby's eyes met across the crowded floor and recognised in one another true soul brothers.

From the dark of his corner Duncan saw it all and was the first person to reach Oonagh's side to see what had happened to her. With the speed of a winger and the strength of a prop forward he leapt to save the mother of the woman he loved. He swept her into his rugby player's arms and had her inside her waiting car before Saul had even had time to begin to wail. Moments later he and Annabel were speeding towards the Four Seasons, Annabel holding her mother's hands and Duncan staring grimly ahead. Duncan had seen everything and this time Kenneth had gone too far.

'Wha . . .?'
   'Did you see?'
   'How . . .?'
Within minutes the guests at the opening, desperate to have nothing to do with the bashing of Gianfranco

around the head were seen slipping away, discreet and silent, keen not to be caught out by the Milanese police. The only people who stayed with Saul as he sat cradling Gianfranco's bleeding head on his lap were Mimi, Antonio and Gladstone, waiting like children who need an idea to inspire them before they can start a new game.

Antonio shoved Mimi towards Saul.

'Go on, you're a girl. Go and comfort him.'

'Have either of you thought to call an ambulance?'

'I think a waiter's done it.'

Paramedics were already making their way through the gallery, wading through the detritus of the party – trampled rose petals and hurriedly discarded glasses, cigarette ends and one of the cupids who'd passed out from too much champagne and excitement.

Gianfranco and the cupid were both gathered up and taken away. Mimi picked up a half empty glass of champagne and swallowed the contents in one go.

'So? You thought Kenneth was going to kill Oonagh and now he has.'

'Surely not.' Antonio didn't sound too worried.

'You saw her collapse.'

'That doesn't mean anything.'

'What?'

'She was drunk as a lord and hadn't eaten for hours and nobody was paying her any attention. She always does it.'

'Didn't you see Kenneth poke her, though? I'm going to confront them. Those boys have some explaining to do.' Mimi was indignant.

'Calm down, sister mine.' Antonio put an arm through hers. 'Let's go dancing. Oonagh's fine; I saw her breathing. Duncan saved the day, the keen bastard, so there won't be room for any of us at her sick bed.'

'Come on, Mimi. It's early — let's go out and enjoy ourselves.' Gladstone glistened with excitement.

'You've got to be joking. Drop me at the Palace and I'll call to make sure Oonagh's all right before I go straight to bed. I've got work to do here, you know.'

'You poor love. Right, Gladstone — dancing for us and the Cinderella dress had better be put away before lovely Mimi turns into a pumpkin.'

Chapter 6

EARLY morning sunlight struggled through the tightly drawn curtains of Oonagh's room. Like Bette Davis she bloomed in gloom and refused to let the harsh light of day get near enough to her facelifts to reveal her age. Annabel, shattered, was playing acolyte of the moment. Duncan snored, his bulk twisted onto a two-seater sofa in the hall outside, his dark red velvet jacket acting as a blanket. Neither Annabel nor Oonagh had thought to find him something more comfortable.

Annabel had spent all night trying to persuade Duncan that her mother had simply suffered an attack of hypoglycaemia and that nothing more sinister could possibly have happened since there wasn't a mark on her.

'I saw your brother jab her with something.'

'Duncan, you know what a child Kenneth is. He was probably trying to get her attention. He's always prodding her – the more violent the prod the bigger the request. I promise you, you're imagining things.'

'You're the one with the imagination. I thought you all considered me incapable of making things up. I'm the Neanderthal man, remember, the boring rugby-playing accountant with no ability to read anything but numbers in columns.'

Annabel blanched. 'You know about the Neanderthal man bit?'

'Of course I do. And the Incredible Hulk. I'm not deaf.' Duncan tried to cover up his embarrassment. 'Don't worry, I don't mind. I know I'm no fairy-tale hero to look at. And if you believe the image you have of me, you must agree that I couldn't possibly have made all this up.'

'I know, but it's all so far-fetched. If anyone should be nominated for an Oscar for an imagination-free life then it's Kenneth. Where would he have got such an idea in the first place? And why would he want to kill off Mummy? It's absurd.'

'Mimi told you about my seeing him coming out of a dodgy door across the street from my house?'

'So?'

'And that I saw Antonio and Gladstone there too?'

'Antonio told me that he and Gladstone were just keeping an eye on Kenneth and Jean-Luc at a party at this tart's flat. Where's the sinister end to that tale?'

'I wouldn't trust any of them further than I could throw them. I mean, where are they now?'

'I hope you're not suggesting that Antonio should be here worrying about my mother?'

'No. But I am suggesting that he should be here

worrying about you. And what about Kenneth and Gladstone? I would have thought it normal for a son to at least ring up and find out what happened to his mother when she collapsed in front of him at a party. And you'd have thought her boyfriend might be doing a little light caring too, wouldn't you?'

'Oh no, she'd hate him to see her being ill – it's so undignified. And Kenneth hasn't rung because he knows perfectly well that if there was anything seriously wrong with her I would have called him and told him to get his arse over here pdq.'

'Don't you see *anything* strange in his not coming to find out if she's OK himself? I mean, you're all staying in the same hotel for God's sake – he's only a floor away from her.'

'I think it's perfectly normal. He knows I'm here, so he quite rightly thinks there's nothing for him to do. Besides, she's fast asleep, the doctor's seen her and given her a clean bill of health, and there's nothing more to do but get some sleep ourselves. Don't fuss so, Duncan. Sometimes you can be more of an old woman than George. If my mother ever dies she'll be in charge of her death herself. My brother won't even get a look-in on the decision-making process.'

'How can you be so clinical? You're not going to leave her, are you?'

'No, of course not. I am going to curl up on the sofa at the end of the bed and get some shuteye. You should go and get some sleep too.'

Duncan humphed and stomped out of the room to march up and down the corridor, wishing he smoked or had some worry beads to play with and growing steadily more furious with Annabel for her blind stupidity. Eventually he sat on the sofa in the passage and dozed fitfully, waiting for events to unfold. Even if his brain was considered redundant, his bulk could be used to protect Annabel and her mother. And like a child who has spent too long at a party of older people, by sunrise he was so fast asleep that when Kenneth and Jean-Luc finally came to visit their victim he heard nothing, saw nothing, and the only sound he made was the gentle snore of an exhausted bear.

'Oh darling, not there. Put them over on this table where I can see them.' Annabel had replaced the water in the vases of Oonagh's funereal selection of white lilies.

'Here?'

'Left a bit.'

'Like this?'

'Right a bit.'

'Mummy, they're fine where they are. Now, how are you feeling?'

'A little fragile, I must admit.'

'I'm not surprised. You put away a ton of wine last night.'

'But champagne usually has no effect on me.'

'Mummy, you're a diabetic. You know drinking is only asking for trouble.'

Oonagh stuck out her bottom lip like the spoilt child she had become. 'It's not fair. I must have the odd little pleasure; there's so little left to me at my time of life. It's your fault for letting Saul open all those bottles before I'd even had time to go home and change.'

'It was his party, Mummy. I couldn't really have suggested that he wait until my dipsomaniac mother was no longer there before he opened up the bubbly, could I? You're hardly forty years old. If you looked after yourself you'd probably live for another forty years. But at the rate you're going you'll die of a rotten liver before the diabetes gets to you.'

'I'm not a dipsomaniac.'

'That's what you say.'

'Where's Gladstone?'

'I've no idea.'

'Well, you might have asked him where he was going.'

'Mummy, I hate to tell you this, but I don't think he even came back here last night.'

'I'm sure he did. It was just that that monolith was lurking like a bodyguard outside the door and wouldn't let him in.'

'Don't be mean. At least Duncan cares about you. Mimi rang to ask after you and I heard Gladstone and Antonio talking about night clubs in the background. How could Gladstone be so careless when you're so ill?'

'Darling, how lovely for them. Of course they like night clubs – they know you're looking after me and they know equally well how I like to hear about the new places

to go to. And as for that Duncan – well, really. He does-
n't even speak English. Where did you find him darling?
And isn't it time he went?'

'Mummy you know perfectly well that I have to have a
Duncan to run the business for me. They're all the same –
you can't get more amusing business managers. I know it's
difficult but you'll just have to put up with him like the
rest of us do. Besides, he was the only man strong enough
to carry you to your car yesterday evening. Gladstone
couldn't have done it and Antonio wouldn't. So thank
your lucky stars that I keep the Neanderthal man at my
beck and call for when you collapse on us.'

'Humph.'

'Agree with me.'

'No.'

'Oh Mummy – grow up!'

'What do you mean? I could have died last night and
I'm just hanging on here by the skin of my teeth and all
you can do is tell me to be nice to a man you admit is as
dull as dishwater.'

'Which reminds me – here's a basin and your tooth-
brush.'

'What for?'

'Well if your beloved little chestnut ever returns you
don't want to breathe fourteen hours of life or death experience all over him do you?'

'Oh really. Do you have to be so explicit?'

'Besides, you never know, make yourself attractive
enough and next time you collapse at an opening your

own boyfriend might rush you to the safety of your hotel bed instead of my business manager.'

'You're not expecting me to go all grateful now are you?'

'Mummy, I don't for a moment think there was anything more seriously wrong with you than there usually is, but it was Duncan who leapt to your side during the emergency. Kenneth just looked dumbstruck . . .'

'Emotion.'

'Jean-Luc just admired Rory's corset from a small height and Gladstone looked shiftier than a pending avalanche.'

'Wrong colour, darling.'

'Oh but so much more chic than a mud slide don't you think?'

'Which reminds me.'

'What?'

'We have to get Kenneth away from that Jean-Luc. You know he makes Kenneth spend all his money on clothes only so that he can wear them.'

'A mortal sin.'

'Well, start with the wardrobe and the subsequent possibilities are endless.'

'Is this all you're really worried about? Mother, I give up. When are you going to realise that you are a ridiculous old hag who has made herself so unlovable that it's a miracle she even knows her son well enough to complain about his boyfriend. I am going to work and you can lie here and wait for your fan club to visit.'

'But who's going to guard the door?'

'I don't know, darling – but it's time Duncan got some sleep so he's coming with me.'

The door slammed wide. Kenneth posed, unsuccessfully negotiating a basket of forced lily of the valley and a bottle of champagne through the opening while trying to do a Hollywood stunner in the doorway. He looked more B movie drag queen, but Oonagh appreciated the effort he'd made.

'Mummy!'

'Darling!'

'What happened?'

'You mean why aren't I dead?' Kenneth blanched a little but nevertheless advanced bravely into the room. He didn't have much choice: Jean-Luc made his retreat impossible. Annabel groaned and made for the door.

'Come on, Duncan. Let's get out of here. I'm not hanging around to witness this little piece of theatre.'

So Duncan, groggy with sleep, followed Annabel up the stairs until he realised he'd followed her right to her hotel room door. Blushing, he apologised and turned away, but Annabel didn't even notice. She was already shouting at the recumbent Antonio and Gladstone who were snoring, still dressed, on the matching pair of sofas in her sitting room.

'What the hell do you two think you're doing here?'

'What?'

'Get up and get out. Do you know what time it is?'

'What are you talking about? We only got to bed about a minute ago.'

'Well, it's time to move it, both of you. I've got a long day ahead of me and I need some space to get ready for it, and unlike you two I haven't had any sleep at all.' Annabel stood, headmistressy hands on hips, and waited for them to move.

'Do you really love this girl?' Gladstone groaned at Antonio as he rubbed his eyes and struggled to a sitting position.

'Stop asking stupid questions and go and check on my mother. Kenneth and Jean-Luc have just turned up to ask after her. She'll throw you out if you don't show the proper attention.' To Annabel's astonishment, before she'd even finished her sentence both Antonio and Gladstone had shot to their feet. 'Where are you going?' she wailed.

'Nothing for you to worry your pretty little head about, my baby. Back later,' called Antonio as he shoved his arms into his leather jacket and searched in his breast pocket for his sunglasses.

Annabel stomped into the bathroom, furious. She hadn't really wanted to get rid of Antonio, and he should have had the nous to realise it.

If Annabel had gone straight to the showroom instead of to her own hotel room for a shower and some breakfast, she would have found George fluttering in an advanced state of anticipation round the buyers from Neiman Marcus, who were fingering Annabel's collection and gleaming with exitement. Mimi was making the most of the opportunity to sing Annabel's praises and skip two shows in the process. She schmoozed the buyers with such skill they thought they might offer her a job. Little did they know that her blood was running cold at the thought of being fired for not covering the shows she was missing. Gloria had a volcanic temper and Mimi was not simply risking her opportunity to shoot Annabel's collection for the magazine but her whole career as well. Her fear gave her sales technique a nervous energy that even the most over-budget department store buyer would be hard put to resist.

George waved at the racks arranged on three sides of their corner of the gallery with one of the brand-new order pads which he and Duncan had spent hours fighting over. George was delighted with the result – the three carbon copies were in pleasing shades of rose, fuchsia and scarlet, and George's exquisite copperplate handwriting had been used instead of ordinary printing. He was as keen to show these off to buyers as he was to show the collection.

'I think the must-have is a piece from each theme in the collection. That way your shop floor will tell everyone all about Annabel's genius and you can see quickly which pieces sell.' He smoothed a fabric sample book which had taken him a whole night in the London atelier to make. 'As you can see, everything comes in a selection of colours, and some of the fabrics are interchangeable. Of course, everything was dyed and woven specially for us.'

'Hmm . . .' The buyer fingered one of the dove-grey dévoré evening dresses and didn't look overly impressed. He looked disparagingly at the price list and commented, 'I thought we'd just perhaps take one or two evening pieces and see how they go.'

'No, with the greatest respect, I think you'll find you need some of the day pieces to make up the narrative.'

'Really? You are good at telling people how to do their job, young man.'

'George is right,' Mimi interrupted. 'Gloria was telling me only yesterday evening that the key pieces of next season are all going to involve felt as in the suits we have here, dévoré bias-cut dresses as we have here and sharp-shouldered military style overcoats as we have here.' She smiled benignly through her lies. 'I'm not sure you have any choice.'

'But the price!'

'Oh, it's hardly in the same league as the other lines you carry.'

'That's beside the point. The other lines are names. If you charge me three fifty sterling for this dress I'm going to have to sell it at around the two thousand dollar mark when you add in the sales tax. I'm just not convinced the general public are going to pay that kind of money for a name they've never heard of.'

'Yes, but the general public never darken the doors of your designer rooms, do they? Anyone who reads my runway report will know that Annabel is a name that's come to stay and that if they're going to be even remotely chic next season they're going to need at least one Annabel piece.' Mimi was warming to this lying lark. She might be going to shoot the collection, but Gloria could (a) cancel the shoot at any time before it was actually done, (b) perfectly easily bin the pictures as soon as she saw them or (c) keep it as a filler for a mid-season magazine and not print it in the collections issue. Also, Mimi had absolutely nothing to do with the runway report, but Mimi was the most loyal of friends and would lie her way into eternity if it meant getting Annabel's line into big American department stores.

'Who else has bought for the States?'

George rushed for his sales file. 'Alan Bilzerian in Boston, they took a concept collection – you know, one of everything just to see how it goes – Bergdorf's.'

'What did they take?'

'Party dresses,' George admitted.

'Oh, so they're allowed to buy only tiny quantities and you'll make me buy like Bilzerian, who's the only store in Boston and therefore has a captive market.'

'Not quite the same, I'm sure you'll agree. But we have sold well in New York, across the collection. Why don't I give you exclusive for certain areas of the States – San Francisco perhaps – and then you'll have to take the whole collection?'

'Hmm . . . The overcoats would do specially well there, wouldn't they?'

'San Francisco society does travel in the winter. Just because the temperature doesn't get low enough for big coats on the coast I hardly think that San Francisco clients are likely to hole up in their first houses and never visit Europe during the winter. You must agree.'

'Must I? All right, young man. Stop waving the order pad at me like some kind of weapon. We'll take a 38, a 40 and 42 in the pink party dresses that look as if they're made of lining material; we'll take the same sizes in the khaki suits – and no, we don't want the pants before you ask – and we'll take one 38 in the greatcoats with the pale pink lining; and then a 38 and a 40 in the Pandora grey dévoré. Don't try and sell me another thing and give me ninety days to pay and you've got a deal.'

'Ninety days! We'd be bankrupt if we gave a soul ninety days. Pay on delivery, just for this season. You'll be a sell-out in a matter of days, I promise, and then next season we can renegotiate.'

'Fax through the order and I'll think about it. When do you need the confirmations?'

'ASAP?'

The buyer sighed. 'All this negotiating gives me a headache.'

'Not as bad as the one I hear Gianfranco's got.' George thought it prudent to change the subject before the buyer had time to realise that he'd put in a lovely big order, enough to pay George's salary for three months, in fact, and that cash on delivery was an excellent deal, specially for a new business like this one.

The buyer collapsed onto a chair and began to fan himself. 'I heard that Bobby was paid by someone else to do it.'

'No . . . I thought he was out for simple revenge. After all, it was a bit mean of Saul to dump him in the middle of the Galliano show last autumn – all those people there taking photos. Gay Smith made a fortune.'

'I heard that another photographer who shall remain nameless is trying to get Saul's job at Gloria's magazine and that he thinks that without Gianfranco he'll have a nervous breakdown and do no work for years leaving the coast clear for him.'

'Who is this person?'

'Me, gossip? Never. Come along, darling.' The buyer waved at his frazzled female assistant. 'Time to shop. And perhaps later we'll find time to nip to the Duomo and give thanks for Gianfranco's lucky escape. He must have a head made of steel to have survived that swipe.' With that they swept out of the gallery, leaving George exhausted but exhilarated by the success of his first big sale.

Jean-Luc leaned back in his comfortable chair at Bice in the Via Borgospesso where he was lunching with Kenneth and Gladstone. The restaurant was buzzing with speculation about Gianfranco's lucky escape, the colour of the flowers at his hospital bedside, whether he really did have a steel plate in his head in case of this type of attack. Everyone was talking about it – except for Jean-Luc, Kenneth and Gladstone. They, naturally, could talk of nothing except the fact that Oonagh had survived a more subtle form of attack and how they were going to remedy the situation.

'You forgot to take ze lid off ze pen!'

'Yes.' Kenneth was relieved that Jean-Luc seemed to understand. The heat of the power he'd felt flowing through his veins before and during the party the previous evening had drained away. Once again he was the mincing little fool with the courage of a rat and the brains of an amoeba who had no defence against the scorn of his boyfriend.

'You mean you made me support you, polish your ego, virtually carry you srough customs and drag you to zat party, and you forgot to take ze lid off. I don't believe ziss.'

'Well, it's understandable, isn't it?' Kenneth was desperate that Jean-Luc would forgive him for his failure to murder his mother. 'You saw, didn't you, Gladstone? I mean, everything happened so fast, didn't it? And when Bobby arrived and I saw what he was going to do written all over his face I thought that then was my perfect moment because nobody would notice in all the mess, and because I was in a hurry not to miss the moment, I forgot to take the lid off the pen. Gladstone, you do see, don't you?'

'Kenneth, only a complete dimwit could have failed in his mission yesterday evening and you, I'm afraid, have proved yourself a dimwit extraordinaire. In fact, I think I'm going to ring Steven Jones in London and order a Dunce Hat for you so that all the world will know better than to trust you with the smallest commission.' Gladstone wiped tears of laughter from his eyes.

'No, don't. I'm not that useless. Please, boys, understand what I'm trying to do here. I mean, when was the last time either of you tried to kill your mother?'

He had a point. Gladstone and Jean-Luc didn't concede it.

'Darling, zere was no reason for me to murder my muzzer. She was very dull, very poor, and she died years ago before I had time even to sink of ze idea.'

'Exactly. You're not killing your mother for the sake of murder. You're doing it for the money and because you think it'll make Jean-Luc love you forever. It's an existential, altruistic act. The choice was there for you to make and with our help you picked the right road and failed to reach the pot of gold at the end of the rainbow.'

Kenneth's brow creased in his effort to swim through the sea of mixed metaphors being thrown at him. Gladstone waved a menacing bread stick in Kenneth's direction and continued remorselessly.

'I mean, imagine, if she carries on as she is at the moment there'll be nothing for you to inherit. You'll be bright young baronet living in a squat on a condemned council estate somewhere trying to fight off gangs.'

Kenneth shuddered at the thought and pushed his cold lobster around his plate like a child negotiating for tinned spaghetti. He sighed and stuck his bottom lip out. 'I don't think it would have worked anyway,' he said.

'Darling, don't try to sink.' Jean-Luc patted Kenneth's hand. 'Sinking was never your best asset. You just wait for me to come up wizz ze next plan.'

'But . . .'

'Please, darling – you'll only waste everybody's time.'

'Oh, please listen to me.'

Jean-Luc pursed his lips and whistled a little tune. 'All right – say your piece but don't be upset when we tell you you're talking rubbish.'

'The insulin probably wouldn't have worked because she was absolutely plastered.'

'Why?' Gladstone was curious.

'You see, I'm not that stupid.' Kenneth stuck his tongue out at Jean-Luc, his courage returning. 'She collapsed anyway – it was nothing to do with me shoving a lidded syringe up her arse. She was hypoglycaemic already. She needed the insulin. She always does this. If she thinks she's not getting enough attention she "forgets" to take her medicine and then when she collapses one of us has to take care of her. So you see insulin isn't going to work.'

'You've forgotten that it's much stronger insulin than she should have. You said it'd kill her in an instant.'

'Well, I was wrong, I think – especially if her blood sugar level's already unstable thanks to her determined lack of attention to her condition.'

Gladstone grinned at Jean-Luc. 'You know, he might have a point.'

'Oh really? Of course he hasn't.'

'Admit it, Jean-Luc. Your beloved little Kenneth isn't that stupid.'

'Yes, he is. But I'll concede 'e might 'ave a small point. I expect 'e's been researching or somesing. Only I can't imagine when. 'E's always wizz me.'

'The point I'm trying to make,' said Kenneth, looking

thoroughly pleased with himself, 'is that we're going to
have to find another way to do it.' He took a large gulp
from his crystal glass and inadvertently dribbled a little on
his double damask napkin. Heat and power began to
course through his veins again. He attacked his lobster
with renewed vigour and said with his mouth full,
'Evidently, not only do I have the balls to do this thing but
I'm not as stupid as you lot think. Leave it to me. I'll
come up with a better plan.'

'God help us,' Gladstone pleaded with the pictures on
the restaurant walls.

'You . . .' Jean-Luc could feel the determined energy
pulsing from Kenneth's eyes. 'You are going to come up
wizz your own plan for ze murder of your muzzer?'

'Oh, don't be so explicit.'

'Well, if you're so ballsy you shouldn't mind.'
Gladstone was laughing again. 'You two are such a wonderful double act. And I'm supposed to be keeping an eye
on you. If only I believed you for one second – you'd be
behind bars in a flash!'

'You'll be laughing on the other side of your face,
Gladstone, when I succeed in my mission. Are you jealous, Jean-Luc? I'm sure we can find someone for you to
do away with if you're feeling left out. My goody good
sister for instance, or that Neanderthal man who follows
her about like an Andrex puppy's parent all day long.'

'Zat will be unnecessary. Really. I wasn't planning
blood bass.' Jean-Luc was offended.

'Only trying to help, darling.'

'Well, if you're so full of ideas today, what's your plan for the next attempt?' Gladstone sat back in his chair watching Kenneth and Jean-Luc. It was like watching a bad American mid-afternoon soap when these two were around.

'I have got an idea, actually.'

'Ooh! Actually you have, have you? Well, spit it out, darling, and we'll shoot it down later.'

'Shh – not another word. Spics are about.'

Annabel had decided to take Duncan out to lunch to reward him for his help with her mother and to apologise for shouting at him when he had suggested that Kenneth had tried to poison Oonagh. They walked into the restaurant and were ushered to a table barely ten feet from her brother. She groaned.

'Hello, boys. You'll forgive us if we don't join you. Business to attend to.' She blew a kiss in their direction just to show willing and settled down behind her large menu, her tastebuds drooling over thoughts of risotto Milanese and large portions of politically incorrect veal.

Mimi's heart made such a noise she thought it would deafen her as she turned the handle of Kenneth and Jean-Luc's room at the Four Seasons. In the gloom she couldn't tell if anyone was there. She tiptoed across to the bed and looked, her heart thumping louder by the minute. If the boys were sleeping she would surely wake them up simply by being in the same room as them. Silence. She drew a sharp intake of breath as she saw a lump on the bed which

could easily have been a body, and leaned forward for
closer inspection.

'Antonio! What the hell are you doing here? This isn't
your room.'

'Huh . . .' He sat up rubbing his eyes. 'What time is it?
Where've you been all this time?' And then a startled
'Mimi! What are you doing here?'

'I might well ask you the same question.' She stood
hands on hips, and waited for his answer. He rolled over
and reached for cigarettes in his jacket pocket.

'I'm keeping an eye on those boys for Oonagh.' He
snapped his lighter shut. 'And you?'

'A great eye you're keeping. Not only were both of
them firmly shut, but the boys aren't even in the hotel.'

'I expect they'll be back soon. Anyway, I had to get
some sleep. I didn't sleep at all last night, and Annabel
threw me and Gladstone out at some unearthly hour
this morning. I just had to get a bit of shuteye. Kenneth
and Jean-Luc are hardly going to start murdering people
in broad daylight, are they? Besides, Gladstone's taken
them out to lunch somewhere, so don't shout at me
please!'

'All right, I'll stop shouting. As long as one of you's
preventing them from doing Oonagh in then I suppose
the other can sleep. Was Annabel all right this morning?
She wasn't too upset?'

'What about?'

'Her mother, stupid.'

'Her mother's perfectly all right. No, she was just he

usual bossy, fussy self. When she told us that her dear mama was alone with the boys, Gladstone and I rushed down to check on Oonagh, like the responsible grown-ups we are, and I haven't seen her since. I expect she's boring herself to tears with the Incredible Hulk somewhere and calling it work.'

'You're such a charmer sometimes, Antonio.'

'Realistic, I'd call it.'

Mimi marched to the windows and opened the curtains, revealing the wreck of the room around them. 'Wow, and I thought I was untidy.'

'Yeah – impressive, isn't it?' Antonio reached into another pocket in his jacket for his sunglasses. 'They even told the maids that they didn't want them to clear the room up, I don't know why. Privacy, I suppose.' He lay back and blew smoke rings at the ceiling.

'Or because they have something to hide.'

'What do you mean, something to hide? Those two are positively transparent. With the best will in the world I can't imagine how they'd ever find anything worth hiding.' Antonio looked at his sister with interest. 'How did you get in here?'

'Tried the door, silly, and it opened.'

'Shit.' He stubbed out his cigarette. 'Well, now you've woken me up I may as well go and find those two twits and find out what they're up to.'

'Antonio . . .'

'What?' He shrugged on his jacket and reached under the bed for his shoes.

'Do you think Kenneth and Jean-Luc will try something on Oonagh?'

'Aha! The truth will out. You are lovely, my little darling. I didn't even have to wheedle what you were doing here out of you.'

'Why should you? I thought I saw Kenneth jab Oonagh with something last night, just before she collapsed. I'm looking for evidence if you must know. I realise you couldn't care less and long to do nothing but check out the local night life, but I'm different. I shouldn't have let myself be persuaded to go home without coming here to check on Oonagh first.'

'You rang and Annabel said she was fine.'

'That was just Annabel being kind so I could get a good night's sleep.'

'Kind, Annabel?'

'Yes, Antonio! Stop being so stupid. I know you know how kind she can be or you wouldn't want to marry her, would you?'

'Nah. I'm doing it for her generosity of spirit – absolutely.'

Mimi couldn't ignore the sarcasm in her brother's voice. 'You can be a cruel bastard sometimes.'

'I have to keep in practice. Annabel would leave in a flash if she thought I actually liked anyone or anything.'

'So you really don't think there's anything going on?'

'I told you last night that Kenneth says he's going to kill Oonagh, but you know as well as I do that he's physically and mentally incapable of carrying it out. Come on. I'll take you to lunch if you like. I bet you haven't eaten.'

'Don't need to. I've got to lose a stone before I can fit into any of Annabel's model's pieces. Lunch is out for the moment.' Mimi made her way towards the bathroom. 'Besides, it's Versace in half an hour. I thought you'd been invited. I think Donatella loves your South American swarthiness, you know. I expect she wants you and Antonio Banderas to sit next to each other and wow the photographers.'

Antonio smoothed his skintight white T-shirt over his pecs. 'She may well do. Yeah – come on. I'll give you a lift. I've got Oonagh's car while she's receiving visitors at her death bed.'

'Death bed! You do think he was trying to kill her, don't you? Wait. I want to check for clues before we go anywhere.'

'Oh, choose life, Mimi. Come on, there must be more to this afternoon than rifling through Kenneth French's washbag. Yuck – at least I hope there is.'

'Hi!' a breathy little voice said from the door. Mimi turned and saw Bobby Frisco tossing his beautifully coloured gold and copper locks at her and grinning. 'Is he here?'

'Who?'

'Kenneth the dreamboat, the manna from heaven, the answer to all my prayers. Don't tell me he's not here. I brought him a present.' He held out, like an offering at an altar, a tiny little Bulgari box.

'No, he's not here.' Mimi looked puzzled. 'Aren't you supposed to be in prison for attempted manslaughter?'

'Bail, darling, and a little baksheesh. So popular with these Italian police. How else do you think they feed their families? Not on their salaries, certainly. I shouldn't think they'll ever bring the case to court.' Bobby perched in a tiny space between piles of luggage on the edge of the bed. 'But I'm prattling and we've never been formally introduced.' He held out his hand to be kissed by Antonio and said in a dusky and undoubtedly false New Orleans voice, 'Bobby Frisco.' He smiled and batted his eyelashes at Antonio. 'It's a delight.'

Mimi laughed at Antonio's embarrassment. Bobby didn't drop his hand, so she shook it and said, 'Lovely to meet you, Bobby, but we've got to go. It's Versace in twenty minutes and I'll really be for it if I don't turn up. Another time.' She took his arm and tried to get him to leave with her.

'No. Don't worry. I'll wait for him here. Don't fret,' he giggled capriciously, 'I'm hardly going to steal anything, now am I?'

Mimi looked at Antonio for guidance. After all, he had been the first person to break into the room. He could decide whether they should leave someone there.

'I don't care what you do. Help yourself to as much of this crap as you like. As if any of it's worth taking.' Antonio took Mimi's hand, a habit formed in childhood when they had joined forces to get out of trouble. 'Come on, Mimi, let's leave the Bulgari package to do as it will.'

And so another day in the life of the Milan fashion week continued. After lunch Annabel and Duncan went to the showroom to check on the sales and found George in full flow and thrilled with his success as a sales person.

'I think I'm going to have to leave you, Annabel.'

She blanched. 'Why?'

'I'm just too good at this stuff. Three of the buyers have offered to take me out. I'm sure they want to poach me.'

'Poison you, more like. Why would they want to give you their jobs?'

Duncan was shocked. 'Don't be mean, Annabel. I expect George is very good at selling.'

'That's beside the point. He's pretty good as my assistant too. I won't have you leaving me, George.'

'Panic not, my darling Annabel. I won't leave you, I promise.' George turned to Duncan. 'Blimey! I never realised she cared.' Duncan noticed that George's hands were shaking as he pulled out a kirby grip to secure his wayward fringe.

Annabel continued implacably. 'I just thought we were a team, George. When we set up this company it was on the understanding that everyone would give at least two years of their time to it before they even thought about taking stock.'

'Was it?' said Duncan. 'I don't remember anything like that in George's contract. Stop it, Annabel. Look – the poor thing's terrified you're going to sack him for making a joke!'

'Well, I didn't notice anyone laughing. Loyalty isn't contracted, Duncan, it's just – well – an agreement. I didn't contract it because I thought everyone understood.'

Duncan stood back and eyed Annabel for a moment. She was exquisite in a little boxy jacket and cigarette pants made of sari fabric, pink shot with orange. On her feet were lilac shantung ballet shoes and over one arm a lilac shantung bag, small enough for a mobile phone, a credit card, a pack of cigarettes and a lipstick.

'Understood what exactly, Annabel?' Duncan's voice was calm as Lake Windermere two days before a storm.

'Understood about the loyalty I expect from everyone. I mean, if I'm prepared to make sacrifices for this company then I expect everyone else to as well. We're a team, and together we make collections which I hope will sell worldwide. We'll all make our names.'

'Right.'

'I don't understand what you're looking so cross about.' Annabel was beginning to bristle.

'Calm down, both of you, will you?' pleaded George, increasingly embarrassed by the scene he seemed to have caused. 'I can't see why either of you is getting ants in your pants. I might, just might, go for a drink with a dreamy buyer, but I'm not leaving the company. You know my loyalty is with you, Annabel. You know that I agree with *Women's Wear Daily* and think you are the next Elsa Schiaparelli. You know that I'll stick with you like a whole factory of glue and hopefully we'll all get to the top together. And Duncan, of course Annabel expects loyalty. How else could she possibly be expected to operate?' He took Duncan's arm. 'We are privileged enough to be working with genius. A bit of respect is deserved, don't you think?'

'I'm sorry. I evidently misunderstood.' Duncan looked unrepentant.

George giggled nervously. 'Don't you think you ought to kiss and make up?'

Duncan blushed. Annabel was already in another corner of the display, rearranging the slightly wilting roses on the hem of a party dress. 'I don't think she cares, George.' He headed towards the door. 'Annabel, shall I check on your mother for you? I can see you'll be tied up here all afternoon. I'll call you and let you know how she is.'

'Thanks. You're sweet.' Annabel didn't even turn to look at him.

Duncan was not tempted by the Versace show, the Versace party, or any other kind of hem-spotting event. His thoughts were firmly elsewhere. He took a cab back to the Four Seasons and, having checked on Oonagh who was holding court with Saul and a bandaged Gianfranco as her audience, he slipped up one floor and strolled nonchalantly along the corridor to Kenneth and Jean-Luc's room. Their voices carried clearly through the door.

'Ugh, but Kenneth, 'e can't stay 'ere. Apart from ze fact zat 'e wear Eau Sauvage which make me retch, 'e 'as nowhere to sit, no? We 'ave ze Versace party to get ready for. What is 'e going to do while we do zat, huh?'

'Shut up, Jean-Luc. If he wants to he can stay. It's not every day I'm given Bulgari cufflinks. It would hardly be polite to ask him to leave now, would it?'

'But . . .'

'I tell you what – I'll take first shower, then I'll go and talk to Bobby in the bar. I know how long it takes you to get the youth back onto your face. We'll wait for you there.'

A door slammed and Duncan edged away. He wasn't sure what he'd expected to find in Kenneth's room, but it certainly wasn't Bobby Frisco, a man out on bail for attempted manslaughter. From the sound of it, he was a new member of Kenneth's team.

Duncan marched back downstairs, wondering what he'd been doing snooping in the first place. He wasn't sure what he had expected to find. After all, he would hardly have broken into the room and gone through Kenneth and Jean-Luc's things in search of poison, would he? He headed for the bar. There was nothing for him to do here except drink, and so he would, and put it on Annabel's precious company money too. How dared she speak to George like that? He'd put money on her not even having bothered to find out that this was George's first trip abroad in an aeroplane. George was perfectly well aware that Annabel needed to sell more than projected because she had gone over budget, and so instead of repairing torn hems and generally keeping the collection in pristine condition he'd launched himself into international fashion sales in order to save her skin – while she swanned around lunching with people. Duncan chose a dark corner and planted his navy Armani-clad frame in an armchair too small for his back and too low for his legs. They had to be hooked around the side of the table, and he would have to move them all the time if the bar started to fill up. With any luck everyone would be going to some party or other and he could quietly get drunk on his own.

He ordered a large gin and tonic. His huge hands closed over a tiny bowl of mixed salted nuts and he swallowed the contents in one go. Annabel: ever more puzzling and ever more attractive. He smiled to himself. He'd nearly got really angry with her this afternoon. But George was right. She did have a right to expect a certain loyalty from them all, even though it wouldn't hurt to show a tiny touch of gratitude every now and then. He finished his drink and waved for another. Poor Duncan had failed to grasp an essential tenet of the fashion world: everyone, from parasites to true creatives, was expected to work their socks off, twenty-four hours a day, three hundred and sixty-five days a year, and they should never expect any gratitude.

Duncan sat alone in his dark corner and contemplated his life. Fortunately Kenneth and Bobby arrived soon enough to prevent him giving in to terminal melancholia. They ordered strawberry daiquiris and sat at the bar giggling and shouting and generally showing off.

'Darling, they are too divine.' Kenneth shot his pale pink Paul Smith cuffs and waved them at the barman. 'Aren't they divine? Don't you think so?'

'Oh, I don't know. I mean, I like them. Do you *really* like them?' Bobby's Southern accent came and went like waves upon a New Jersey beach. 'The boy in the store had me look at all of them. He wanted me to buy you the diamonds, but I said, "Why diamonds for a man who's really a pearl?" See, they're black pearls and the gold is just as heavy as it can be. Do you really like them?'

'Of course I do. That rat Jean-Luc never gives me presents unless I give him money.'

Bobby smiled as if he understood everything. The fact that Kenneth's excitable conversation jumped around like static on cashmere straight back from the dry-cleaners didn't bother Bobby one bit.

'Oh, you poor thing. I don't see why you hang around with him. He's so old.'

'Darling, he's thirty-three next birthday.'

'It shows, honey – his colourist is having to work hard on the grey.'

'Colourist?'

'He does colour his hair, doesn't he?'

'Oh, yes, of course he does. He's trying to look like me.'

'Impossible, you're a natural. He's just a fake. I swear, there are thousands like him in those dirty little bars round that Pigalle place in Paris. Drop him and he'll disappear there quick as a flash. It's not that he won't be trying to make an impression, it's just that there are so many of them buzzing round people like you like bees round a honey pot, if you'll pardon the expression.'

'Not at all. I've never been called a honey pot before.'

'Where have you been all your life?'

Duncan grimaced into his third gin and tonic, part of him fascinated by this exchange. Had Jean-Luc been dumped; would Bobby take his place as chief page of the

Baron French's bedchamber; would Kenneth bring up his mother's collapse of the previous evening? The questions were endless. The crucial one, however, was, did Duncan care? Then Kenneth moved the conversation onto more interesting ground.

'So what came over you? Did you plan to kill Gianfranco? Or was it just a ruse to get your own back?' Kenneth's face shone with curiosity and a desire to learn.

'Oh, what a disaster! Darling, I had every intention of killing him, of course I did! And when he sank to the ground I felt that my finest hour must have arrived. But honey, that man must have steel plates in his head. Did you see the angle I got him at? A heavy blow to the right temple – he should have been dead as a doornail.'

'You're too delicate, perhaps.'

'Oh, you're too kind. Darling, I'm strong as an ox, and usually with a baseball bat in my hands I bear more than a passing resemblance to a bull in a china shop.'

'You mean you've done it before?'

'Hundreds of times. Practice makes perfect, you know.'

Neither Bobby nor Kenneth heard Duncan splutter into his drink. He'd definitely prefer Kenneth to stick with Jean-Luc if Bobby was to be this kind of influence on him.

'Quick, head down!'

Duncan looked up to see what Kenneth was hiding from and saw Mimi framed in the doorway squinting slightly through the gloom. Seeing him, she smiled and came across to his table.

'Hi.'

'Hi. Can I get you a drink?'

'Thanks, I'll have a vodka martini. Versace shows always make me feel like glamorous movie drinks, the sort of thing you'd never even think of usually.'

'Vodka martini it is then. Do you want me to add the shaken not stirred bit when I order it, or don't you mind?'

'I only have it shaken when it's made with gin.' She smiled at him, her generous mouth wide with pleasure at having him to herself for a while. 'I'll take it as it comes, thanks.'

Duncan ordered and then turned back to her. 'How's it going?' He was genuinely curious. Perhaps Mimi could throw some light on all these strange people dressed in uniform pink.

'Good. I think. I'm glad to see Kenneth's found a suitable new friend.'

'Yeah, they've been making so much noise I'm surprised no one's brought in a policeman to arrest Bobby for all the other murders he's claiming as his own.'

'Really? Oh well, while he's showing off, Kenneth can keep him out of trouble, can't he?'

'Now there's a thought — Kenneth as probation officer. I'm sure he'll be a great success.'

Mimi sipped thoughtfully at her cocktail. 'Mmm . . . I always forget how delicious these are. Do you think they'd bring us any nuts if we asked them? I skipped lunch in an effort to diet and now I must eat something, or I'll get terribly drunk, throw up all over you and not enjoy this little break at all.'

'Break? More work this evening?'

'Two more shows and the Versace party. Are you going?'

'You've got to be joking. I felt such a fish out of water last night, I'd rather swim around here inhaling gin and tonics as fast as they can make them for me. Besides I've only got one party dress and I wore that last night.'

'So? I've only got one myself. I'm proving that if the dress is good enough its narrative will stay fresh for as many days in a row as you need.'

'What?'

'Never mind. Let's say I'm setting a trend. This season my trademark is pink and orange Prada. And here it is, freshly dry-cleaned and ready for another sortie. Your trademark could be oxblood velvet – a powerful colour, you must admit.' She smoothed the Prada mousseline and looked at Duncan's miserable face. 'Do you hate it all that much?'

'I just don't understand it, that's all.'

'It's only clothes, Duncan. And everyone here's either buying or selling them. It's that simple.'

'So why do they have to make such a noise about it? I nearly had a fight with Annabel this afternoon when she suddenly turned all princessy on George, demanding things of him which frankly she has no right to. You know, he works his socks off and I've never once heard her thank him. Come to think of it, it's not often she thanks anybody.'

'But that's because this business means so much to her.

She gives one hundred per cent commitment and expects the same from everybody else. She thinks it's not worth doing otherwise.'

'Meanwhile people are out there killing themselves for her and she can't even say one word of thanks.'

'She will, you'll see. Once you get back to the UK and this circus trip round the world is over she'll give a big party to thank everyone in the atelier.'

'She will?'

'I promise you, Duncan. You're not getting all disillusioned on her, are you? You know, Paris is going to be three times worse than this. It's longer, there are more shows to fit in per day, there are more parties that you're going to have to go to and everyone's that much more on edge because they're all exhausted and secretly beginning to wish it was all over – and then there's New York.'

'Don't remind me. I'll be a nervous wreck by the time we get back to London. And then I've got to get the first year's accounts in order.'

'Oh, don't be so down in the mouth. Don't the Inland Revenue give you a few weeks' grace as you're a new company?'

'I doubt it. I expect they'll come down on us doubly hard to try and get rid of us – less work for them if we're not around. Perhaps we should move all operations to Milan. Apparently all the Italian designers are being sued for not paying their taxes for the past millennium.' Mimi laughed. 'This whole industry must be a joke. Come on, let me get you another drink before you go back to work.'

'How kind you are, Duncan. Thank you.' Her jet-black eyes twinkled at him with the only friendly lights he'd seen in a long time. Grateful? He'd have asked her to marry him — if he hadn't been in love with Annabel, of course. 'And while you drink yourself into a drunken stupor try and remind yourself that the fashion world isn't the be-all and end-all of everything.'

'I meant to ask you about that. What is it with this world thing? Other industries are called just that. They don't have a world to themselves. Who are these people who think that they move in their own private hemisphere, and that the hoi polloi can lurk outside it like those shoals of tiny fish that hang around great white sharks or killer whales?'

Mimi looked at him, suddenly a little irritated. 'You don't have to do it. If you think this little world of ours is so out of touch with the real world then why don't you get out there? I'm sure other people are lining up to give you jobs.'

'I'm sorry. I've upset you. I shouldn't be drinking so fast. I have a bad habit of saying what I really think after three gin and tonics.'

'I'm not upset really. But we're all here making a living. People may look to you as if they're self-obsessed, or at least fashion obsessed, but this is what everyone who's in Milan this particular week does. And I think they're lucky to be so enthralled by what they do. I certainly think I am. I can't imagine anything worse than having to go to a job I wasn't interested in every day, just so I can pay the bills. I thank whoever is in charge that I've got the chance to earn a living doing something I really love, and fly round the world and meet interesting people and . . .'

'Interesting!'

'Glad you think you're so dull.' Mimi giggled at Duncan's grumpy face. 'Come on, Mr Neanderthal man, lighten up.' She finished her second drink and got up to leave. 'You know, Annabel might be right. You can be a bit whingey sometimes.'

'I'm not whingeing. I'm just trying to make sense of what's going on, that's all.'

'Well, don't rush it, darling. You only got into this business eight months ago. You can't expect to understand it in a week. I tell you what – I'll send you over some biographies of Chanel, Balenciaga, Christian Dior and Schiaparelli for you to read to start your education. Might that make things easier?'

Duncan grinned at her. 'Go on, go to the party. Don't worry about educating me. I'll just sit here and quietly turn into an old soak.'

'Stay here long enough and I'll be back later and you can tell me what Bobby and Kenneth get up to in my absence.'

'I doubt it. It looks as if they're coming to beg a lift off you.'

'Oh God! Why didn't I make my escape earlier?'

PART 3

Paris

Chapter 7

It was raining when the Annabel French cavalcade arrived in Paris. The pavements outside the Hôtel Saint Simon were slick and greasy, the taxi driver from the airport more than usually aggressive and unhelpful, and George was nearly in tears because he'd lost the pink feather boa he'd come to think of as his lucky charm. Also he was tired, homesick and in need of a real cup of tea, suffering the disorientation of the Englishman abroad for the first time. Annabel, on the other hand, was in the best of spirits. After all, the horse chestnuts and the plane trees were in bud, the Place de la Concorde still felt as if it belonged to her alone, and a gracious taxi driver would have confused the issue and made her feel much less at home.

'Come on, everyone!' she cried, lugging the first of the coffins full of clothes out of the boot of the first car. 'What are you all doing? We've got to get a move on. I'm having dinner with Cristo tonight and we've got to be all set up by then. I'm not spending an evening next to Gloria Wharton and Don Elson without having something absolutely perfect to show them tomorrow.' Duncan helped heave the rest of the baggage out of the two taxis it had taken to transport them all from Charles de Gaulle airport.

'Come on, George.' Annabel hadn't even noticed George's air of melancholy.

'Gloria's already seen it,' a little voice said from the car.

'But Don hasn't, has he, darling? And we wouldn't want to piss off the most powerful man in glossy magazines, now would we?' Annabel's tone was brisk and perhaps a teeny bit icy.

'Leave it, Annabel,' warned Duncan. 'The poor thing's exhausted. Why don't you go and book the three of us in? George needs a bath and a rest. I'll get the rest of this stuff sorted out.'

'Oh, you can be so masterful sometimes, Duncan.' His heart lurched out of rhythm at the brilliance of her smile. Sometimes Annabel was so beautiful that it quite took his breath away. Did she press a switch inside herself somewhere to turn a light on? And why did she always do it when he was really annoyed with her?

'Come on, Georgie,' she cried to the interior of one of the taxis, any ice in her voice replaced by a tap running warm caramel sauce. 'Duncan says you're tired and emotional and need to eat, sleep or go to the loo quickly, and

I think he's probably right. Which do you want to do first? Come on, this hotel is like a second home to me. Whatever you want, I'll show you the way.' She disappeared into the little eighteenth-century hotel that was her special haven when she came to Paris. She much preferred being a big fish hidden in a small pond in the left bank of Paris than a stickleback celebrating overnight success in the huge sea of the Four Seasons in Milan.

With a proprietorial air she dragged George up to his room, a miniature work of art off the courtyard, lined with pale yellow striped taffeta and furnished mostly with a huge bed and a tiny cupboard of a bathroom. George sank gratefully onto the bed. He wasn't used to Annabel being so caring and intended to make the most of it before she remembered herself.

'How about a burger, chips and a large cold beer?' she asked, already dialling room service.

'Mmm . . .' was all the answer he could manage.

'Can we have a bit more enthusiasm, please?'

'MMMmmmm . . .' George said, upping the volume a bit.

'That's more like it. Now then.' Annabel installed herself on a straight-backed, uncomfortable chair, beautifully upholstered in sunflower-yellow and white ticking. 'What's the matter, George? Duncan's right. You do look as if all the stuffing's been taken out of you. Is this something a burger and chips will cure or should you be talking to Auntie Annabel about it?'

George laughed weakly. 'You'll think I'm pathetic.'

'Darling, the state you're in at the moment I already think that. Come on, tell me all about it. As long as you don't mention money or leaving me for some large American conglomerate then I promise not to fight with you.' Annabel batted her eyelids at him over her shoulder as she went to answer the door. 'Aha! Food! We'll see what this does for the morale around here.' She put the tray on the bed, snapped open two bottles of Becks, removed the silver dome covers from the plates with a flourish, poured liberal quantities of tomato ketchup over both portions of chips and finally looked up. 'Well?'

'I've lost my feather boa.'

'Wha . . .?' she said through a mouthful of chips.

'And nobody loves me.'

'Oh well,' said Annabel swallowing hard. 'Not much I can do about that, is there? But if you like I'll take you to Le Marié and we'll get you a new boa at the same time as ordering for next season's collection.'

'It's a start.' George sighed and looked nervously under the bun of his burger. He couldn't flirt with Annabel as she liked him to when he was this shattered. And he hated all this chummy one minute bossy the next business. She was his employer, not his friend. He didn't trust her.

'Generosity is my middle name, George, as you well know. Right.' Annabel stood and wiped her mouth. She'd inhaled her burger rather than eaten it. 'When you've had a shower and sorted yourself out a bit we'd better go and set up. How long do you think you'll be?' She looked pointedly at her watch. Evidently she'd like to go immediately.

'An hour?' George asked nervously.

'I'll meet you downstairs in forty-five minutes. I can't imagine what you need an hour for.'

After Annabel had left, George pushed aside the remains of the food he'd hardly touched and lay back on the bed. What would she do if he didn't turn up in three quarters of an hour? Pushing himself up and towards the shower he decided it wasn't worth thinking about. He'd better just be there. After all, there were thousands of eager beavers who would be happy to take his place. He needed the tiny amount of money that Annabel paid him. And, like Mimi, in spite of complete exhaustion, he was deeply relieved every day when he woke up that he didn't have to do a job he hated to pay the bills, but instead got to practise being a designer himself while trying to earn a living.

'And this is Madame de Pompadour, my mother's dog.' Kenneth kicked the Pekinese out of the way as he showed Bobby Frisco through the huge apartment on the Champs de Mars where he'd lived with Oonagh for the past five years. 'Don't worry about her. But don't let Mummy catch you kicking her or you'll be out on your ear faster than a fast thing.' Kenneth giggled at his own wit and opened the door of the salon where Oonagh lay in splendour on an ugly Victorian chaise longue, the only jarring note in the elegantly proportioned room. Four sets of French windows along the west side gave a view of plane trees and the Eiffel Tower, framed by the watery blue clarity peculiar to the Paris sky in March.

Madame de Pompadour scampered through Bobby's legs and leapt onto Oonagh's lap, hiding her head under the protection of her mistress's arm.

'Oh darling, are you shy of our little Bobby? Don't be so timid, sweetling, he won't bite. Will you, Bobby?' Oonagh took the dog and held her up for Bobby to take and stroke. Madame de Pompadour tried and failed to take a chunk out of Bobby's hand and Bobby leapt back.

'Ow!'

'Oh, don't be fussy, darling. Madame de Pompadour didn't touch you, did you, darling? Not for lack of trying, though. Isn't she a brave little thing? But you're timid, aren't you precious, a little nervous of strangers. Never mind. I'm sure you'll soon be the best of friends. Now.' She sat up and rang a little silver bell on the table beside her. 'Tea, I think. And business, of course.' Oonagh revealed her teeth in an attempt to smile at Bobby. 'I believe that Jean-Luc's long-term arrangements have changed. Have you sent his things on, Kenneth? Not that he had much,' she added, turning to Bobby. 'Poor thing, he came with nothing and with very little he goes away. Still, you can't take it with you, can you?'

'I'm sorry?' Bobby was confused.

'When you die. You can hardly pack in readiness and have a little cash set aside in case your baggage is over-weight, can you? No, much better that he go back where he came from with nothing of ours. After all, what use will he have for all those lovely clothes and jewellery in Pigalle? It's all bound to be stolen from him within a

atter of minutes and then he'd be left with nothing.' She
urned back to Kenneth. 'But you did give him that little
heque I gave you for him, didn't you?'

'Yes, Mummy, and you'll never guess what he did with
?'

'No, darling. I can't imagine it was anything more
xciting than rushing down to the nearest post office to
pen an account with it.'

'Oh no, nothing so sensible. He tore it up and put the
eces down a grating in the street outside the Four
asons and said he had no need of charity and that he'd
ade other arrangements.'

'Oh, I expect he's made a new friend. How inconve-
ent. I suppose that means we might still see him around
om time to time.'

'I doubt it. I think he was just furious.'

'Spitting tacks,' interrupted Bobby. 'I saw him do it. It
is funny. I don't think I've ever seen anyone so angry.
onestly, he was a foolish boy. It's not as if he and Kenneth
re married or anything. I mean, what did you really
e him, Kenneth?'

Kenneth blushed slightly. 'I can't imagine.'

The conversation was suspended while Oonagh's maid
sumpta arrived and poured tea into Sèvres cups from a
er tea service which Oonagh had whipped from her
d husband's ancestral home, now sold to be a prep
ool. Kenneth watched his mother offer Bobby biscuits
e perfected his new scheme to get rid of the barriers to
estate. Gladstone and Antonio had to go. Jean-Luc had

already gone, and Bobby wouldn't cost half as much as h
had. And then he had to get Annabel disinherited. Th
way he could bleed his mother of his own money and th
coup she'd thought impossible would have been effecte
with minimum murder and maximum profit for Kennet
He smiled at the thought. Thank goodness Bobby ha
arrived at the right time. He'd help Kenneth achieve h
ambition and wouldn't boss him around like Jean-Luc di
Kenneth looked at Bobby fondly. At that moment th
salon door was pushed open, and the cosy domest
tableau was broken up.

'Gladstone! Antonio! How gorgeous.' Oonagh ra
for more tea and missed the looks of distaste her lov
and her daughter's boyfriend shot Bobby, who show
off his gold right incisor in response to their glares a
didn't move up to make room for one of them on t
little two-seater Second Empire sofa he was occupyir
Gladstone and Antonio installed themselves at either e
of the fireplace like a pair of unlikely latter-day Evel
Waugh good guys and obediently accepted tea. Th
weren't planning on staying long. They'd passed by simp
to check that Jean-Luc really was out of the picture a
that Bobby Frisco had been installed in his place. Bobb
proprietorial grasp of the sofa left them in no doubt as
the redesignation of roles, and as soon as they could th
tried to get away.

'Oonagh, darling, we have to go.' Gladstone bent a
stroked his mistress's cheek.

'Why?' Her tone was as imperious as usual.

'Annabel needs help setting up at the Bourse and we
romised we'd go over there and see what we can do.'

'She can't need both of you. Antonio, you go. You are
pposed to be her boyfriend, after all. But Gladstone,
u must stay. She's already got the Neanderthal man and
eorge to help her. I can't imagine what she'd do with
th of you.'

'But we promised, Oonagh.' Antonio kissed her on
th cheeks and headed for the door. 'You know how fond
e is of Gladstone,' he lied, 'and she's hardly seen him
ce the collections started. I expect she'd like to take us
r a drink later and we can all catch up.'

'I thought she was dining with Cristo tonight.'

'And so's Antonio.' Gladstone joined his partner in
ime in the doorway. 'But I'll be back. Why don't we go
d eat at the Ritz tonight? You book, Oonagh. As we
en't going to Cristo's but everyone else is, there should
room for us. It'll be fun, no?'

Oonagh sighed. 'I suppose so. You'll come, boys, won't
u?' She looked enquiringly at Kenneth and Bobby.

'Of course, Mummy. We'll have a lovely time.'

'Good. That's settled then. See you there at about
ht, darling?'

'That's a bit early. Make it nine-thirty. I've got so much
catch up on with Annabel.'

'Ugh – all she'll talk about is figures and what the
credible Hulk's been telling her to do. You'll be bored
id in about two seconds flat.'

'Maybe. But I'd better show willing, hadn't I? You know

how hard she's been working. She needs a few minutes t
relax. I'll see you later.' Gladstone blew a kiss from th
doorway and, arm in arm with Antonio, headed off dow
the corridor to the front door. 'I'm not sure how muc
longer I can put up with the stupid bitch,' he muttere
under his breath.

'Well, it's entirely up to you, my dear boy. You ca
either wait for Kenneth to cause your paramour to po
her clogs or you can actually think of something that migh
earn you a living.'

'Even if Kenneth does kill her off, what right do I hav
to expect anything?'

Down on the *quai* the boys ordered a cab and directe
it to the China Club in the eleventh arrondissement. In th
privacy of the cab they could talk undisturbed.

'Annabel will see you right – I'll make sure of that.'

'Oh, yeah, after she becomes your obedient wife,
course.'

'Of course.'

'It'll never happen.'

'Of course it will – why would she want to turn m
down? I'm gorgeous, I'm tall, I play polo, I'm potential
quite rich and I'll worship the ground she walks on
long as she gives me a nice free rein.'

'I'm not talking about Annabel – I'm talking abo
Kenneth. If he kills Oonagh off – which let's face it
about as likely as him joining Mensa – he'll drop me fro
the family accounts quick as a flash, and meanwhile I'
stuck to her ladyship's coat tails indefinitely.'

'Do something else then. Get her to change the will in our favour, make me executor and then kill her off yourself.'

'Don't be ridiculous,' Gladstone said testily. 'I'm no murderer.'

'Have you any idea what that woman's worth?'

'Roughly.'

A self-satisfied look spread across Antonio's face. 'I went and looked at the land registry last week in London.'

'Just before you decided you'd better actually marry Annabel.'

'Shut up and listen, Gladstone. Do you know how much she sold all that land for when she upped sticks and moved to France?'

'No, can't say I do.'

'OK – the land went for five million and the Sotheby's sale made another three million. Now, this was in the early seventies. With inflation and good management, that's got to be worth at least fifty million now – even after she's bought her daughter a fashion house and spent as much money as she possibly can on you. She's no fool, you know. I go down in her accounts as a non-tax deductible expense. Did you know that?'

'God knows what I go down as then.'

'I should think she excuses you as being medicinal.'

The taxi stopped outside the China Club and the boys headed for the bar. The barman's attempts to interest them in a complicated cocktail he'd just invented fell on stony ground.

'*Je t'ai dit deux bières. Je m'en fiche de ton foutu cocktail.*'
Gladstone turned back to Antonio, who was lighting a
Gauloise. Antonio took a long swig at his beer and
sighed.

'That's better.' He looked at Gladstone with curiosity.
'Do you think Oonagh's in love with you?'

'Nah, she just likes me to play boyfriend. We never
sleep together, or hardly ever. She thinks it's cool to have
a black boyfriend fifteen years her junior. In her opinion
I look good on her arm but I'm totally talentless. It's all
bullshit. I just make her look more ridiculous, and I'm a
good artist. One of these days I'll have an exhibition that
isn't bought and paid for in advance by Oonagh French
Inc. and she'll be stunned by the reviews and have to
change her mind entirely about me.' He shot his DKNY
sweatshirt cuffs (paid for by Oonagh) and his Rolex glit-
tered angrily on his wrist. Antonio ignored this outburst
and Gladstone calmed down. 'So, enough of my money
troubles. When's this rushed marriage and honeymoon
going to happen? Paris has hardly started and we've still
got New York to go. You haven't even had to fight Annabel
off recently, she's been so busy. Bet you never thought
she'd make such a success of herself.'

'It never even crossed my mind she might be any good.
It's bloody irritating. We should be in London now, picking up the pieces of her dashed fashion ambitions and I
could propose to her at any time of the day or night. As it
is, I haven't seen her since the day before yesterday and
unless I take a stand I'll sit miles away from her tonight

Cristo's and she'll be too busy working to administer to my needs until after New York.'

'So do it this evening then,' said Gladstone. 'What's she going to do? She can hardly turn you down, can she?'

'That'll be no good. I'll be seated at the other end of the room, and she'll be next to Cristo so he can get a good look at her and suck all her creative energy towards him. Useless.'

'If I were you, Antonio, I'd take her aside before dinner and get the difficult question over with. She'll be glowing with happiness, and they can hardly prevent a newly engaged couple from sitting next to each other, can they? That way you get to sit next to Cristo too, and be the star of the evening playing the prince-consort-to-be of the newly crowned queen of fashion. I expect when the papers get hold of it the French government will get so excited they'll let you have a licence without a moment's delay so you can get married in the Hôtel de Ville on Saturday morning with *Paris Match* officiating and Chelsea Town Hall's nose being put firmly out of joint.'

'Don't get carried away, Gladstone. It's a shame I can't get a ring till I get hold of the money. You don't have access to a cheque book, do you?'

'Unfortunately not, or I'd rush you to Cartier this very moment. As it is you can buy me another beer and help me work out how to do an exhibition, then I can leave Oonagh discreetly with enough money in my pocket to actually live. I've had enough of playing gigolo to that old crone, and I'm bored of Kenneth's antics, and frankly, the idea of sharing an apartment with Bobby Frisco makes me want to throw up. When you've helped me make my fortune through honest toil I'll buy you as much jewellery as you want.'

'It's a deal. Then I'd better go. It doesn't do to be late for Cristo, now does it?'

'Are you picking her up?'

'Who?'

'Annabel, you fool. God, anyone would think you weren't interested in her at all.'

'I'm not,' Antonio said candidly. 'I'm interested in her money. Yeah, I'll pick her up, and in the meantime you can make a plan for this exhibition of yours. We'll talk about it in the morning.'

'I thought you might have a bit more input than that – like where, when, that sort of thing.'

'Hey, I'm no genius,' Antonio protested. 'I've never even seen any of your pictures.'

'That's easy – they're just huge blank canvases covered in stripes of paint with the odd sort of sun or moon shape thrown in for good measure.'

'Sounds like the kind of stuff that'd sell like hot cakes.'

'But where?' Gladstone asked.

'Here?'

'Nah, Paris is much too reactionary for that kind of thing.'

Antonio smiled mockingly. 'Ooh, long words for this time of the evening. London then.'

'Nah. London's full of people doing exactly the same thing. I'd get lost in the competition.'

'I've got it!' Antonio slammed his hand on the bar.

'What?'

'Don't you worry about a thing, Gladstone old man – how many canvases?'

'I don't know – twenty, thirty? I can rustle up a few more in a couple of days if you need them.'

'And they're big, right?'

'Huge. Never smaller than ten feet square – mostly bigger.'

'Cool. Leave it to me. For my measly twenty-five per cent I'll make you independently rich in no time.'

'I'll believe it when I see it.'

'Trust me.'

Antonio stood and drained the last of his beer. Slinging his leather jacket over his shoulder, he arranged his Cutler and Gross sunglasses on top of his head then slapped Gladstone on the back.

'Better go do my stuff with the friendly neighbourhood ice queen. I'll call you.'

'Yeah – later. As long as she says yes. I don't want to know about any more disasters.'

'There's no question of disaster. What would she want to say no for?'

Cristo's party. As *Vanity Fair* said, 'You had to be there.' Cristo lived in one wing of a house big enough to qualify for stately home status. Within the eighteenth-century walls he'd restored and furnished it to perfect pre-revolutionary splendour: the rooms were hung in specially woven Lyon silk damask; the furniture was original and exquisitely upholstered in embroidered silk. The garden, a long narrow stretch of gravel outside one side of the house, had been arranged with a formality which only the French have perfected. It featured box hedges and topiarised yew, and no flowers except in the lichened stone pots which flanked the rows of glass doors. These were filled with early, forced, dwarf white lilac which grew up and over the rims of the pots in a soft cloud of light and perfumed the night with a hint of heaven.

A party given here at any point of the year would have a chic and a glamour which Saul Smytheson, with his pink and gold and collection of paid cherubs, and Gianfranco Desire, with his overheated gardens and lit trays of drinks, could only try and imagine. This dinner was it; the high point of the fashion circus which was halfway through its seasonal migration. This evening would remind everyone why they did what they did, why they tried to make beautiful things, why they designed dresses which only a handful of women in the world could afford to wear. For a few short hours the guests would forget the fact that they had to shoot twenty-five pages of ready to wear in four days, that they had to sell months and months of advertising on the back of their invitation to this party, that the models were just thin, tired girls who wished they could chuck it all in and go to St Barts for a holiday with their boyfriends. When fashion editors shot dinner party scenes with the most beautiful girls wearing the most exquisite dresses sitting at the most perfect tables laid with the very best china, linen and glass, this was what they were trying, and always just failing, to re-create. This was where the dream became reality.

Guests were received in the small drawing room, lit only by great branches of candelabra which had been wound about with ivy and oak leaves, sprigs of thyme and rosemary and pale early anemones which glowed like Annabel's skin, ivory edged with pink. In this rarefied atmosphere even Antonio was a little nervous as he and Annabel were announced by a liveried butler who got away with wearing a powdered wig without looking in the slightest bit ridiculous. Annabel shook hands with Cristo, fighting a desire to curtsey. Antonio bowed with all his South American charm and was kissed on both cheeks for his efforts.

'Thank you for coming.' Their host's English was perfect. He spotted Mimi standing behind them. 'Ah, Mimi! I'm so thrilled you could be here.' Mimi's invitation was due to the fact that she and her mother had been lifetime clients of Cristo's, not to her lowly status at Gloria's magazine. Gloria stood behind Mimi steaming with fury. This little upstart was going to have to go. 'And you've brought your boss with you! How marvellous! I can spend all evening singing your praises and making sure that your inevitable rise to magazine stardom is perfectly understood by our lovely Gloria.' He kissed Gloria on both cheeks. 'Or would that drive you even madder than you already are, darling?' he whispered into her ear.

She blushed scarlet and made for a tray of champagne,

draining her first glass in one go and grabbing another immediately. Her hands shook slightly and she decided that a trip to the loo for a quick line of Charlie might be an extremely good idea. How else was she going to get through this evening? Cristo might be the most powerful man in the fashion industry, but it was hardly in his interest to piss off the most powerful fashion editor in the world – unless he knew that he didn't have to curry her favour. Gloria swallowed hard. Was she really for the high jump? Her boss Don Elson arrived and her suspicions were confirmed. He made a beeline for Annabel and Antonio, having looked through her as if she were a plate of glass, and began to pay court to the current success of the season.

'Honey, I hear you are so it and of the moment that I can't wait to come and feel your collection. Can I come tomorrow? Or even, would you give me a private show after dinner?' Don wiped his nose with a red linen handkerchief and laughed lewdly. 'Don't worry, Ant – I'll not steal her from under you. I know you have squatter's rights with this one.'

'Worry couldn't be further from my mind,' Antonio snarled. 'I'll let you know if I ever do move on and then she's all yours.' He took Annabel's hand without looking at her and led her through a set of French windows and into the garden, grabbing a couple of glasses of champagne along the way.

Once they were safely installed on a weatherbeaten teak bench, Antonio took a quick slurp of his champagne in anticipation of his declaration and turned to look at Annabel. He was shocked by what he saw. Instead of leaning towards him, her eyes wide with expectation and ready to hang upon his every word as she should be, Annabel was sitting bolt upright at the far end of the bench and staring at him with such fury that he wondered why his face didn't burn from the laser beams shining from her eyes.

He uncrossed his legs slowly. Whatever he'd done he'd better make amends quickly if he was to rescue the situation and get the proposal over by dinner.

'Are you all right?' he asked, lighting a Gauloise and sending the smoke in a sharp jet into the lilac-scented air.

'No.'

'Why not? What's the matter?'

'How can you ask that?' Annabel's voice shook with fury.

'Have a drink, Bella – you're obviously very stressed about something.' He gulped at his champagne and put the glass down. 'I'm sorry if I haven't been around much lately, but you've been so busy being the toast of the season I've hardly been able to get through the crowds. Besides, I knew you wouldn't need me about with George and the Incredible Hulk to look after you. I thought it better to keep out of the way. You're not cross with me, darling, are you? I hate it when you're cross – it gives you ugly little lines across your forehead.' He reached forward to stroke the offending lines away but Annabel stood up and started towards the end of the garden, leaving him waving foolishly at a couple of hairdressers gossiping in a doorway. 'Annabel! Wait! This is embarrassing. You can't just walk off like that. What's going on?' Antonio caught up with her and grabbed her arm. She shook him off and turned to the attack, suddenly appearing to him taller and thinner and sharper, and altogether much too reminiscent of her mother.

'How dare you?' she spat.

'How dare I what?'

'I can't believe you don't even realise what you've done.'

'What have I done? Annabel, what are you talking about.'

'Offering me to magazine directors as if I were a piece of meat for sale in a butcher's. Talking about me as if I weren't there. Did you notice that during that little exchange neither of you even looked at me? You just discussed me as you might an inanimate object, something you'd bought and paid for and had the right to do as you liked with.'

'Don't be ridiculous. He was flattering you and I was flattering you back.'

'Flattering! I think your words went along the lines of, "When I've finished with her I'll let you know and you can fish her out of the bin and have her if you like" – the implication being that not only am I yours to throw away but that once you've thrown me I have nothing to do with who might appropriate me next. I'm a person, Antonio, a human being, and I belong to nobody but myself. I'm certainly not yours to do anything with.'

Antonio spluttered. 'What are you getting so upset about? That's just how people talk to each other – I wasn't serious.'

'That's beside the point. How could you be so unfeeling for me? I thought you loved me.'

'I do.'

'Rubbish! You just love yourself, and having me as a girlfriend is only useful so long as I sleep with you when you want me to and make myself scarce when you don't. All that ridiculous stuff about not wanting to bother me during my moment of fame – of course I've wanted you there. Of course I could have done with a bit of support. And I'm hardly going to get that from Duncan and George – they're employees, for God's sake! I can hardly admit defeat and exhaustion in front of them, can I? They look to me to keep morale up, to keep them going until this bloody month of tripping round the world air kissing the same people any number of times in any number of places is over. You could have been there. You could have reminded me that there is more to life than dressmaking and parties. But you didn't even see that. You just kept away, didn't you, spent all your time with that hateful Gladstone.'

'He's all right . . .'

'Don't argue with me, Antonio. Let's face it, you hate the hard work of relationships. You just want me to be there to polish your ego for you in public and private, and when my attention's elsewhere while I'm trying to make a living you just disappear to dingy bars with Gladstone and pretend you're helping me.' She began to stomp towards the other end of the garden, her perspex Manolo heels being fatally scratched by the gravel in the process. For once she didn't even notice.

Antonio watched her go, wobbling slightly on her heels, and once she'd reached the other end of the garden he went into the house to fetch two more glasses of champagne. Fortunately the guests were still arriving. He still had time to redeem himself.

Back in the garden Annabel was perched on a stone step, her tiny pink lining material dress hardly covering anything, hugging her knees to herself and trying to stop her chin from shaking too much. Antonio sat down beside her and handed her a glass of champagne. He lit another cigarette and leant back against an urn.

'I don't know what to say. I've obviously fucked up big time and I'm going to have to work bloody hard to get back into your affections. It's a shame.' He screwed up his eyes and managed a hint of tears. 'I was going to ask you to marry me tonight.'

'*What?*' She jumped away from him.

Antonio stayed where he was, cultivating the watery-eyed look and smoking. 'I love you, you see. I was going to ask you to marry me and then I thought we could have a little wedding on Saturday at the Hôtel de Ville. Oonagh knows some people in the Mayor's office and I thought she'd be able to rush through a licence for us. Since we were in Paris and it was so romantic, I thought it would be the perfect end to a perfect time for you – all your success, and then marriage to me.' He looked up. Something was wrong – she wasn't even looking at him.

'Very good, Antonio. You've just made one tiny little mistake, though.'

'What do you mean?'

'Do you really think you're so wonderful that you are something I deserve now I'm famous?'

'No!' By now Antonio was badly rattled. This conversation was definitely not going according to plan.

'That's what you just said,' Annabel continued implacably. 'You said it would be perfect for me to have success and you. Why couldn't you just tell me you love me and want to marry me? You're sort of keeping yourself out of this, aren't you? I can't marry somebody who expects to be kept on a pedestal and polished and worshipped by me, the little acolyte. And do you really want to be like an award, like one of the awards I'll probably get at the Venus de la Mode? I'd talk about you like that. You know, I'd look back on this year and say, "Ah yes, that was the season I won best newcomer and my prize was Antonio. Wasn't it good of him to lower himself to my level, to grace my mantelpiece with his gorgeous self?" No. I deserve more than that. I'm not sure what you deserve but I know that if I can't have the whole fairy tale then I'd rather not have anything at all.' She stood up. 'They're calling us in for dinner; I'd better go. I'm sitting next to Cristo. You'll be all right – I think you're next to Antonio Banderas. Cristo must have heard how well you got on with him at the Versace show.'

And with that she walked away. Antonio sat, his jaw grazing the gravel. She'd turned him down, flat, and without any sign of regret or emotion. He couldn't believe it.

For years afterwards it was remembered as one of the great parties of the late twentieth century; seventy people being entertained in a manner not seen since the demise of the French monarchy at the end of the eighteenth century. The food was exquisite: langoustines in a warm cream of Coquilles St Jacques sauce; lamb and *chou au foie gras*; poached pears in a caramel sauce with pear sorbet sandwiched between crisp squares of brandy snaps; and cheeses that the French as well as the English, American, Italian, German, Japanese, Australasian and Spanish guests had never even imagined. A different wine for each course gave added lustre to the seven damask-clad tables where the flowers, white lilies and ivy, curled round the glasses and the plates like frames at a gallery for gourmets.

Nobody noticed that Annabel and Antonio didn't exchange a word after their conversation on the terrace before dinner. Even Mimi, being entertained by Rory on one side and a happily recovered Gianfranco Desire on the other, was unaware that her brother's meal ticket had just been torn up and thrown away like Jean-Luc's had been in Milan. Those Frenches were tougher than they looked, and twice as determined. Nobody took advantage of them for too long – certainly not South American lotharios with egos the size of their native country's national debt.

*

'*Mamà* – hello, it's me.'

'Marianita, darling, where are you now?'

'Paris.'

'And are you at the Ritz?'

'No, *Mamà*, I told you, I'm at the Regina. It's OK – a bit old-fashioned, but central, and I've always had a passion for Joan of Arc on the traffic island outside.'

'You were always so gifted at prioritising, darling. How's it going? Is Annabel still the star of the show?'

'Well, Galliano and Cristo are showing tomorrow, and Alexander McQueen the day after. But I think she's standing her ground well. I don't think it'll be the show of the season, but certainly she gets prize for best new-comer.'

'I am glad. I remember her making dresses for her dolls when she was little – do you remember that? They were so sweet and always so prettily done. I'm not at all sur-prised she's made such a success of this. Is it green fingers she has?'

'No, *Mamà* – those are for gardeners. And this isn't really the same as making doll's dresses, but I agree with you it's great that she's so successful. And there's more good news.'

'Yes, darling? You seduced the crunchy accountant?'

'No, don't be silly. I think my boss is for the high jump.'

'How do you know?'

'Well, Cristo gave a dinner tonight.'

'I hope you sent him my love.'

'Yes, *Mamà*, and he says when are you going to be in

Paris so he can do something about your wardrobe for you. He's convinced you're desperately out of date because you haven't been to see him in five years.'

'Oh darling, I've been so busy. Don't tell him I've been dressing in mail-order Ralph Lauren. He'd never speak to me again.'

'Come over for his show. Quickly jump on a plane now.'

'Don't be silly. Your father needs me. His favourite mare is due to foal in the next few days; he's very stressed about it.'

Mimi sighed and sipped at the cognac she'd poured herself. 'Well, maybe I'll order you a few things, just to keep him happy.'

'Fair enough. Now, tell me how you can be so sure that the ghastly Gloria is being put in a sack.'

'*Mamà*, you do these English mistakes on purpose.'

'Maybe I do.' Mimi's mother laughed all the way from Brazil. 'So, tell me the story.'

'It's simple, really – nobody spoke to her all night. She just sat in a corner and was ignored by all and sundry while Don Elson – you know, the group's editorial director – spent the evening schmoozing Nina Charles. I think he wants her to move to Manhattan and take over – I doubt she'd do it, though. She won't admit it, but I think she wants to calm down a bit and have a baby, and now her husband's designed her a house, well . . .'

'*On verra bien*, as they say.'

'Indeed.'

'And how's Antonio? I hope he's looking after Annabel a bit.'

'Completely useless. They managed to have a conversation for about the first time in a week before dinner, but then of course Cristo put Annabel next to him, and he hates straight men, so Antonio was banished to the other side of the room – same table as Gloria, actually – where he was stuck next to Antonio Banderas. They keep being put together because they look so alike and are so gorgeous in pictures. *Paris Match* published one of them at Versace together and captioned it "*Les jumeaux Antonio*". Antonio Ytuarte was not amused. Shouldn't think Banderas was that thrilled, either. I think Antonio's feeling a bit left out now that Annabel has found fame and fortune. She hasn't got a second spare for him.'

'And how about you? Have you seen her?'

'Not really. But I'm shooting her collection in the Parc St Cloud at the weekend and I'm sure she'll come along to make sure I don't fuck up.'

'Language, Marianita, language. So, you have nothing too exciting to report: no advance with the earnest accountant, work's OK, and if you're lucky you'll have a new boss in the near future.'

'No, *Mamà* – things are great. We're over halfway through. I'll be back in Manhattan in less than a week!'

Chapter 8

'SHE fucking dropped me.'
'You can't be serious!'
'You think I'd joke about something like this?'
'What on earth did you do wrong?'
'God knows. One minute she can't get enough of me and I have to fight her off like she's some kind of leech, and the next minute she's telling me cool as a cucumber that I've made a few classic mistakes and she's not interested.'

Antonio drew heavily on his cigarette and finished his third espresso of the morning with a decidedly shaky hand. He was sitting in the Café Flore, the spring sunshine glinting against his sunglasses in the early morning light. It was eight-thirty and the café was almost empty. Only a handful of waiters was there to listen to this conversation, and their faces were uninterested as only Parisian waiters' faces can be.

'Listen, Gladstone, I'm in trouble here. Come over and commiserate or something. I don't know what to do.'

'Don't move. I'm on my way. I'll just go and excuse myself for missing breakfast to her ladyship.'

'I'm waiting. Tell her ladyship to go fuck herself.'

'You've got to be joking. We can't have both of us broke.'

Gladstone struggled out of bed in his studio and padded, naked but for his Calvins, down the hall to Oonagh's bedroom, where she was reading the paper and not eating a breakfast of miniature *Viennoiseries*.

'Darling! How heavenly to see you so early in the morning. Will you join me? Madame de Pompadour always gets too much breakfast – why don't you sit down and join her in her feast?' The Pekinese eyed Gladstone warily and moved to stand guard over the breakfast tray. She had no intention of sharing anything.

'Sorry, honey – can't. I've got to nip out for a moment.'

'At this time of the morning? How unhealthy, darling. You'll have to mix with the hoi polloi and the rush hour.'

'I'll live. Can I take the car?'

'If Marcel's awake enough to drive you anywhere, but I need it back for ten-thirty. I have to be at the hairdresser then. Wasn't dinner last night amusing? I must say, I think this Bobby Frisco a vast improvement on the terrible Jean-Luc. He was always so insipid, and convinced that without him all our lives would collapse. No, I think Kenneth's new friend is charming.' Oonagh said all this while perusing Suzy Menkes' column in the *International Herald Tribune*. 'Look at these pictures, darling. Milan was a disaster, don't you think? I'm so bored with all this pink. It's such a relief to be back in Paris. I'll be wearing ivory to the shows here. What have you got to match?'

'Oonagh, let's talk about this later. I really must go.'

'More secret meetings. Too dull. I'm not sure I shouldn't trade you in for a newer model myself. Perhaps Kenneth's set a trend – perhaps we all need a bit of new blood.'

Gladstone sat down on the edge of Oonagh's bed and gently pushed her still unset hair out of her eyes. 'Would we really be able to live without each other?' he asked, his hand trailing slowly down the scraggy contours of her neck towards her breasts. 'I'm not sure I could.'

Oonagh sighed. 'We'll see, young man. We'll see.' She bared her teeth at him. 'Why don't we make a date for this afternoon – say three o'clock here? I'll let you know after that.'

Gladstone stroked one of her breasts and licked his lips, forcing an expression of lust onto his face. 'Can't wait.'

Ten minutes later, freshly showered and dressed in a black Yohji Yamamoto suit, Gladstone threw himself into the back of Oonagh's car and called Kenneth on his private line as Oonagh's diminutive driver edged the car into the Paris rush-hour traffic.

'Kenneth.'

'What do you want, Gladstone? It's ten to nine in the